CRAZY COVE

A ROMP WITH THE WRITERS OF COURTNEY PARK

Crazy Cove

A Romp with the Writers
of Courtney Park

Editors

Mary Ellen Koroscil
Bala Menon
Sheila E. Tucker

TAMARIND TREE
TORONTO

Library and Archives Canada Cataloguing in Publication

Title: Crazy cove : a romp with the writers of Courtney Park /
        editors, Mary Ellen Koroscil, Bala Menon, Sheila E. Tucker.
Names: Koroscil, Mary Ellen, editor. | Menon, Bala, editor. |
        Tucker, Sheila E., editor.
Description: Essays, short stories, and poetry.
Identifiers: Canadiana 20220177473 | ISBN 9781989242094 (softcover)
Subjects: LCSH: Canadian literature—Ontario—21st century.
Classification: LCC PS8255.O5 C73 2022 | DDC C810.8/09713—dc23

Front cover photo by Reiseuhu on Unsplash
Back cover photo by Claiton Conto on Unsplash

*This book is dedicated to the world's poets, writers and readers:
all lovers of literature. You may find something
of yourself within these pages.*

Contents

PROSE

VERSE

FOREWORD

The mystery of why we write is complex and continuous. Some claim it is for personal gratification, others for fame and recognition and others confirm they are determined to influence opinion. In this lively and eclectic anthology filled with prose and verse, a collection of diverse voices belonging to the Courtney Park Writers join together to mount an impressive testament to the inherent goodness of writing groups and the high quality of literary work this group has produced.

Kim Cayer's short story is told in a colloquial voice that everyone in Canada will recognize. It's about everyday folks who rarely find a voice in literature. Slightly risqué, "The Hot Babes Contest" provides a rollicking start to the *Crazy Cove* anthology.

Trevor C. Trower's "Rabbit Ears" invokes the difference between then and now, those of us who grew up without Smart TVs and digital gadgets, which offer a multitude of choices that cost a fortune. It is a clever tale told in charming language. Trower's next story, "Arf Arf, Woof Woof, Grrrr," reminds me of Garrison Keillor's best *A Prairie Home Companion* yarns and fits perfectly with Mary Ellen Koroscil's engaging personal tale, "Road Apples on Chestnut Avenue," about growing up in Moose Jaw, Saskatchewan.

One of the most moving selections is Konrad Brinck's "The Berlin Airlift: 1947-49," when the 2.8 million inhabitants of Berlin chose starvation over the invasion of the Soviets. Brinck, born after the end of World War II in 1946, recalls the tribulations suffered by his family and how they learned to survive with the help of life-saving airdrops from Britain, the US and France. His personal narrative tells a harrowing tale written in stark language, emphasizing the magnitude of the crisis Berliners faced.

One of Sheila E. Tucker's contributions, "The March," is as frightening as can be: a fictional memory frozen in time and worth reading over and over for its narrative skill. Her other story is a reflection on military families. David L. Tucker's elegant Evelyn Waugh-like excerpt from his forthcoming novel *Picture This!* focuses on the narrator's London reunion with a cousin he hasn't seen in thirty years.

Many of the prose contributions rely on personal experience, stylized and perfected until the narratives from Canada, India, the UK, and Germany are transformed into literature.

The verse in this anthology is as varied and refreshing as the prose. The poems of Pratap Reddy are redolent with meaning, such as these lines from "Karma's Child": *In my declining years, adrift and bereft, / my stash of good deeds now come to nought. / A thousand prayers die on my lips. / For my throat is parched, sore for a dose / of something spiritual, of something sublime.* Or in Reddy's "Writer's Block": *In the distance, slumming with Lake Ontario / Is Toronto / It's late in the evening, / the CN Tower / looks like an upright python / that has swallowed up a flying saucer.*

I am deeply moved by Serina Lewis' poem "The Circle," where the poet relies on Hindi spirituality to write: *Let us not forget... / the herbal healers / the toddy tappers / the tireless helpers / the singers of mandos / the soothers of the lonely / the dreamers from foreign shores / the birthers of successive generations / the youth who wrote letters for their elders / each one leaving footprints indelible on Mother Earth.*

The poetry and prose in this anthology are to be savoured, enjoyed for their originality, refined technique and for how they shift the heart and mind toward the memorable moments in life.

Joyce Wayne
Oakville, 2022

Joyce Wayne is the author of two novels, The Cook's Temptation *and* Last Night of the World *published by Mosaic Press. Her essay, "All the Kremlin's Men," originally appearing in* The Literary Review of Canada *is anthologized in* Best Canadian Essays 2021.

1. INTRODUCTION

Nothing beats a cozy haven where wannabe and established scribes gather to share their ideas, experiences and written work. Many cities, towns and hamlets boast of having a crème de la crème writers' group, and in most cases their illustrious members hail from someplace else.

Our group's name, Courtney Park Writers, is derived from the many years when we met at the Courtney Park Library in Mississauga, Ontario. However, for the past three years we have been meeting in our members' homes or gardens.

I'm proud as a peacock of our group. I credit Cheryl Antao-Xavier for having the wisdom and the withal to have established the Courtney Park Writers many years ago. Later, she handed the reins to me. Our group has been in existence for more than a dozen years and it has been my pleasure to be Chair for the last decade.

Our members inspire and encourage each other to continually improve their craft. Some are natural-born poets, others dream up a collection of short stories, and yet others publish novels or creative nonfiction. Hats off to those who have contributed their ideas and written work that has been woven into the fibres of this anthology.

We are a diverse group, hailing from various parts of the world and from across Canada. We all eventually settled in Ontario. Our origins are part of the glue that keep us together as a creative whole.

To introduce you to the members published in this anthology and to illustrate our diversity: from the United Kingdom are Trevor C. Trower, Rena Flannigan and Sheila E. Tucker; from Europe are Konrad Brinck and Ivy Reiss; from Pakistan we have Zohra Zoberi; Bala Menon, our publisher, hails from India as do Pratap Reddy, Geeta Krishnamoorthy, Meena Chopra, Kumkum Ramchandani and Serina Lewis; and Tasnim Jivaji is from South Africa. Roy Marques originates from South America. From across Canada are Ken Marvell, Linda Cassidy and Joann Wanda Rossitter (Quebec); Doris Grant and David L. Tucker (Ontario); Kim Cayer (Manitoba); and myself, Mary Ellen Koroscil (Saskatchewan).

Collectively, these plus additional members, some quite new, make up our family of writers. I want to thank each and every one of them for contributions to this anthology as well as their support during our meetings, and for enriching my life. Over the years this group has continued to motivate me.

A heartfelt thank you goes out to Sheila E. Tucker, my editing partner; she is my rock. I couldn't have put together this collection without her. I'm so appreciative of our publisher, Bala Menon of Tamarind Tree Books, and thank him for believing in us. He contributes so much to our group.

I hope that you, our readers, enjoy the unique assortment of stories and poetry represented in our anthology. I only wish we really did have the 'crazy cove' our book title suggests. It is a metaphorical place for gathering, and would be our "secret club house" reserved just for us—writers and poets—to share our experiences, our thoughts, to laugh or cry, to read our work and listen to others, and to regale each other with funny tales. It would be a place of camaraderie, where we could laugh out loud.

Mary Ellen Koroscil
Chair, Courtney Park Writers

2. INTRODUCTION

I discovered the Courtney Park Writers by happy chance about four years ago, and am delighted to have joined such a cosmopolitan circle so close to home. Here, the white sands of *Crazy Cove* are strewn with sparkly pink pebbles warmed by the sun, immortal fossils embedded in rock, and curlicue seashells sitting askew. These, respectively, symbolize our fiction and nonfiction prose, as well as the poetry within these pages. Take a stroll along this beach of life. Reach for a piece of dried bladder wrack seaweed and pop it, skim a flat stone across the sea's surface, walk with us as we tell you our stories. Then, spread a towel and lie in the warmth. Our wish is for you to relax and read, and to see your reflections in the water.

Sheila E. Tucker

Courtney Park Writers member and editor

PROSE

KIM CAYER

The Hot Babes Contest

Shawn and I weren't meant to last, but in the three months we dated, he was instrumental to my finding a job at the cool place he worked. Ashcan Aeronautics was located on the airport grounds and since I had a thing for airplanes, this was nirvana for me.

Near the end of our relationship I was invited to a celebration in honour of Ashcan's quarter-century anniversary. Guests of the mostly male employees toured offices and the gigantic hangar where they manufactured aeronautic components. The walk ended at their cafeteria. I hustled to the table where a guy was handing out baseball caps to commemorate the company's milestone.

I was admiring the flashy silver airplane logo on the hat, and barely had the cap on my head when I heard a child's voice ring out. "Mommy, is that lady naked?" I saw the child pointing to a newspaper clipping mounted on the wall.

The man handing out the caps laughed. "No, son," he said. "That's just one of the Hot Babes. They're in the paper every day. But maybe that beige bikini was a bad choice…"

It was quite a display of Hot Babes. Since it was May 25th, there were probably twenty-five photos posted there. I read *The Daily News* that morning and this gorgeous "Stefania," in the barely-there bikini had not been today's Hot Babe. I recalled today's model had been wearing a hockey jersey. I scanned the bunch of clippings and found her at the bottom.

Maybe it was the disappointing sex later that night that led me to pick a fight with Shawn. In a catty voice, I asked him about the cafeteria's decor. "All those half-naked women on the wall," I mused. "Don't you think that makes Ashcan a sexist workplace?"

Shawn disagreed "Today's Hot Babe was all covered up. And she wasn't that good-looking either."

I was startled. "When did you become so interested in the Hot Babes?"

"It was just that the company was hoping for a real "hottie" today because of their party."

I huffed, "I bet the women who work there find the cafeteria so tacky."

Shawn was dressed and looking for his car keys. "Two women work there and they don't eat in the caf. The boss's secretary is his wife and they go out for lunch every day. The other is Selena. She's pregnant. She brings her lunch and eats at her desk. She's ready to pop any day."

"I saw her! She's huge!" I replied. "Hey, if she's going to have a baby, she must be taking time off. Are they looking to replace her?"

Shawn was already at the door. "I dunno," he said. "I'm not in management; I just rivet parts together. You gonna lock up behind me?"

He gave me a goodbye kiss with more passion than he'd shown during our time in bed. Shawn was cute as hell, built like a Greek statue, had a wicked car, a tidy apartment and a decent job. Still, he just wasn't cutting it as boyfriend material.

Monday morning, I phoned in sick at my job with Boutang and Sons Trucking, the company my father had inherited. Dad had no sons. My older sister basically ran the company and loved it. I was a Girl Friday. Not the best job in the world, but I was paid well. After turning my phone off, I headed back to Ashcan Aeronautics. I asked the overly pregnant receptionist if I may speak to Mr. Ashcan and was allowed entry into the boss's glorious office. The walls were overwhelmed with photos of vintage aircrafts. A miniature model of an airplane caught my eye.

"Look at that!" I exclaimed. "A true representation of the Avro Arrow! I can tell—it has the word Aeronautic misspelled."

That drew a smile from both Mr. Ashcan and his wife. "That's right," he agreed. "It's missing the letter 'u'."

"You look familiar," Mrs. Ashcan remarked. "Haven't we met before?"

I nodded. "Yes, at your party last Friday."

"Right, you're Shawn's girlfriend," Mr. Ashcan nodded. "I like him; he's a good worker."

"The reason I'm here is Shawn told me your receptionist is due any day. I was wondering if you'd lined up a replacement?"

"We were just making a help-wanted ad."

With that, I went into a song and dance worthy of an Oscar telecast.

Mr. Ashcan asked, "So you'd be willing to leave your father's business? I'm sure the pay wouldn't be as good." I shrugged. "What does your Dad think?" he continued.

"He knows I prefer planes to trucks," I said. Through his office window, a jet could be seen taking off. "You get to watch Boeing 707s? You've got the best job in the world!"

Mr. Ashcan reached into his desk and pulled out some papers. "You certainly seem like a good fit," he said. "But we're not big on office relationships..."

"You mean, Shawn?" I asked. "We're through. No big deal, it was a mutual thing." Note to self—remember to tell Shawn we broke up.

"Why not fill out an application?" Mr. Ashcan offered. "We'll let you know in a week."

The door burst open. The receptionist hung onto the doorknob, a panicked look in her eyes.

"Selena!" Mrs. Ashcan exclaimed. "What is it?"

"I'm not due for two more weeks," Selena gasped. "But my stomach is hurting so bad and I just had a big accident at my desk..."

"Your water broke," Mrs. Ashcan declared. "Arnie, call 911. Selena, settle down and call your husband. Tell him I'll go with you to the hospital and for him to meet us there." I liked how this woman took charge; perhaps she was the driving force in the company's success. She pointed a finger at me. "Elise, is that your name? Get behind the desk," she ordered. "Until you do something to screw up, you've got the job."

My first duty was to clean up the mess behind the receptionist's desk and find a new chair. At noon the boss said, "Let's go to the cafeteria. I need to cast my vote." I followed Mr. Ashcan. At the cafeteria counter, he said, "I'm sure you weren't ready to spend the day here, so lunch is on me."

I asked for a take-out container of macaroni and cheese. Looking around for my boss, I spotted him at the wall of Hot Babes. He was kidding around over today's model. I sauntered over and heard him say, "She really isn't that attractive. I like a more wholesome look in my women."

His employee countered with, "Well, never mind how she looks, Mr. A. That's probably one of the best bodies that's ever graced the paper!"

"I'm going back to the office," I announced.

"I'm eating here," said Mr. Ashcan. "It's been years since I sampled the food."

He didn't know what he was missing. That mac n' cheese was so delicious, I thought about ordering it on a daily basis. This meant I'd be returning to the caf to get to the bottom of this Hot Babe thing.

The next day, I ran into my ex-boyfriend. He asked if I wanted to join him for lunch. As we both dug into our macaroni, dripping with long strings of cheese, a man resembling Albert Einstein walked by, balancing a cup of tea.

"Did you place your vote?" Einstein asked. "It's the end of the month, I'm tallying up the score."

"Yeah, I did it during my coffee break," Shawn replied. "Go, Destiny!"

"Oh, I disagree," Einstein said. "My vote is on Kathryn." He walked away, still dipping his tea bag in and out of his cup.

I snorted. "The newspaper girls."

"Yup," Shawn acknowledged. "The guys vote on who they think will win Hot Babe of the Month."

"It just seems wrong. We're at work! Women come into the

cafeteria too!"

"Not really," Shawn disagreed. "Not till you came along. Whenever Selena would come in, she didn't seem to mind."

"Well, I don't know if I like it," I pouted.

"Tell that to Mr. Ashcan," Shawn suggested. "It was his idea of team bonding. We like it. It makes for good conversation."

"Oh, right, 'did you see the hooters on the Hot Babes today?' Or 'she's got a great body, shame about the face'."

Shawn cut in. "We take it a step further; we submit our vote to the paper. That gives us a say in who they pick for Girl of the Month."

"Oh, wow," I said sarcastically. "Aren't we becoming upstanding citizens here at Ashcan?"

Shawn stood up to leave. "Boy, am I glad you broke up with me."

It wasn't that I disliked the Hot Babe feature of the paper. You could look if you wanted ... or skip that page. Hell, even my sister once appeared as the Hot Babe, back when she was a Toronto Argonaut cheerleader. However, this was a professional business. How could I ignore all the scantily-dressed women posing on the wall? Today, thirty-one gals smiled lasciviously at the cafeteria patrons.

I decided to put up with this stupid contest for another month. Selena was enjoying maternity leave, and her job was being handled capably by me. Too bad about the niggling aggravation of a human resources issue; otherwise I'd be loving this receptionist position. I sure didn't want to lose this dream job but sooner or later, I was going to file some kind of complaint.

Then the unthinkable happened, with a text from Charlize, my sister. "Look at the last page of *The Daily News* today." I was in line at the local coffee shop when I spotted a copy of the paper. There smiling up at me was Charlize with her dazzling, pearly whites. Her long hair was windswept and her body was shown off to great advantage in the polka dot push-up bra and ripped denim shorts.

I called her. "What are you doing as a Hot Babe?" I wailed.

"Gee, I thought you'd be happy for me," was my sister's reaction.

"I am, it's just that at work ... oh, never mind," I said, not wanting to explain Ashcan's obsession with the Hot Babes. "Why did you do it again when you were already in the paper before?"

"Yeah, back when I was a baby," Charlize retorted. "I just wanted a better picture. Do you like it?"

"It's amazing," I told her. "And you gave Boutang and Sons a plug!"

Charlize laughed. "Perhaps being the Hot Babe will be good for business."

When I went for my morning break there was my sister's photo, with three metal workers gawking at it. "Gotta say, she really has a nice figure," one guy said.

"Really?" I asked. "Do you have to be so nasty?" Lunchtime came. I could smell the macaroni and cheese on the employees who came into the office so I went back to the cafeteria.

I saw Shawn standing at the Hot Babes wall, telling everybody he knew today's Hot Babe. "She happens to be the only sister of ... lo and behold, here's Elise now!" Suddenly, the attention turned to me.

"I see beauty runs in the family," said Einstein. I blushed.

"Seriously, your sister is gorgeous," said a guy whose uniform read "Rajinder."

Various flattering comments were made. I spotted the three metal workers and, approaching their table, mumbled an apology for my earlier outburst. I really wanted their votes.

Charlize appeared early in the month. The next day was a photo of a woman who needed to see an acne specialist, a hair stylist and a dentist. Her picture seemed to make everything right with the world. However, the day after, disaster struck. The Hot Babe was so outrageous, her photo attracted a crowd of men. I squeezed into the bunch for a look. "Belinda" was beautiful. She was hanging upside down from a stripper pole, all her body parts heading south.

"Check out the body on that girl!" A technician exclaimed.

"Quite the rack! And a nice smile," a mechanic remarked.

"How can you see her smile?" I retorted. "Her...rack covers her bottom lip!" The men noticed me standing among them.

"Don't worry," Einstein said. "Your sister is still leading the votes."

"Yeah, but tough competition," I said, with an unexpected hangdog look. "You guys vote how you see fit."

I actually found myself becoming quite involved with the Hot Babes contest. Every day, I'd make my way into the caf for either my coffee or mac n' cheese. I'd surreptitiously check the status of who was in the lead for Ashcan's pick of Hot Babe of the Month. Belinda's photo was odd; she was upside down next to all the other gals. She remained a strong contender for second place. Although other shapely, pretty girls graced the pages of the newspaper, my sister Charlize remained in top spot.

On the day of reckoning, Einstein collected final votes. I anxiously awaited the afternoon break when the winner's photo would be posted in the frame. On the last day, workers had a chance to change their votes if they wished. I actually felt nauseous enough to forgo the usual lunch and opt for a salad.

When the afternoon break rolled around I entered the cafeteria. Sunrays penetrated the picture windows and illuminated the frame hanging on the top of the Hot Babes display. I could see a head, not feet, so I knew Belinda didn't win. I felt better, but not as great as I felt when I approached the display. There, with her winning smile and curvy pose, was my sister's picture.

I burst into tears. You would have thought I won the contest. I placed a call to Charlize. I didn't tell her anything. I invited her for lunch and wanted to surprise her. She agreed to meet me next week.

Upside-down Belinda was the general public's vote for Hot Babe of the Month. The guys at Ashcan had all voted for my sister. The men, in their own weird way, were making an attempt to bond with me. As I waited for Charlize to show up, I stopped Mr. Ashcan and his wife on their way out to lunch.

"Hey, Boss," I said, "do you think I can vote on the Hot Babes contest?"

"I think that's a grand idea," his wife answered. "That contest needs a woman's input. Give some votes to those poor girls who may not be all that attractive, but who are law students or entrepreneurs. Seems the exotic dancers always win."

"Not last month," I grinned. I couldn't wait for my sister to see her framed photo.

Charlize showed up minutes later. After a big hug, she stood back and took a look at me.

"I haven't seen you in two months," my sister said, "You must have gained twenty pounds! What are they feeding you here?"

Damn that mac and cheese. Just when I was thinking I might pose as a Hot Babe.

KIM CAYER

A novelist and professional entertainer, Kim has a short story that was featured in *The Courtney Park Connection*. In addition of having an Amazon e-book called *Dirty Numbers*, also published was *Lights! Camera! Dissatisfaction...* and *No Fire Escape in Hell*. Her next book, *Kitty Casino*, is launching in 2022 with Tamarind Tree Books.

TREVOR C. TROWER

RABBIT EARS

I was shopping at the big department store just south of Highway 401, in Mississauga.

This is because I was so tired of paying my telephone company one hundred and thirty nine dollars a month for our phone and TV service. Now, they had the gall to increase the charges to one hundred and forty two dollars and seventy-five cents for no apparent reason. I want to follow my neighbour's lead and purchase my own antenna.

I remember back in the Fifties when the whole business of television started, we had an indoor antenna. It was a small, wire aerial, which picked up "snowy-looking" local stations. I figured with all the improvements in technology, the reception would be vastly improved. Back then, we used to call that antenna "rabbit ears" and it saved us all a great deal of money.

After I had made my regular purchases, I approached the sales clerk in the TV department. She smiled at me and said, "What can I do for you?" She was a nice-looking young woman wearing a hijab.

"Hello," I said, "Are you the TV salesperson?"

"Yes. What can I help you with, sir?"

"Well," I began to explain. "I am inquiring if a set of rabbit ears would work on a new TV set?"

She stared blankly at me for a moment, then she looked around the store. I immediately thought she was about to call another assistant to help. She backed away slightly. Then in a quiet voice she muttered, "How could rabbit ears possibly help with a television signal?"

I began to inform her how, back in the day, we would place the rabbit ears on the top of the TV and connect them. Then we could twist them about until we received a good signal. Sometimes it would be necessary to pull out the ears and stretch them as far as they would go. We could also bend a coat hanger, and occasionally that would serve the purpose when the regular rabbit ears fell apart. In the midst of relating this history lesson, her smile quickly disappeared and she had backed away from me by several feet. I smiled at her and said in a conversational way: "My present TV system is able to provide me with approximately two hundred channels; however, none of them are really worth watching."

Then I noticed the other employee, who was older and had been standing in the same area, near us. She was carefully watching this transaction and had moved closer. I detected a slight smile on her face. She seemed to be enjoying the consternation of the younger woman.

In a cheerful voice she added, "Oh yes, we used to do the same thing, in fact we all used rabbit ears, in the early years of television."

Then the clerk explained to the younger assistant that they weren't real rabbit ears, but that it was the term used for a device— an aerial, which we referred to as rabbit ears as a nickname.

It was sort of comical to see how the young woman's facial expression changed. She relaxed as she realized I was not some cruel sadist with an unusual proclivity. And now she had a better sense of what I was looking for. Then, alas, she advised me that they didn't carry them in stock.

TREVOR C. TROWER

Arf Arf, Woof Woof, Grrrr

The sound of a barking dog can eventually drive a man mad. Like the Chinese water torture or being forced to sleep with your eyes open. Systematic and continuous noise for one, is often unheard by the dog-fancier. How is it that the owner of the barking dog doesn't hear the grating, abrasive sound, when the neighbours suffer lack of sleep waiting for the tuneless noise to stop? My poor friend Ray needed his sleep; however, for several nights in a row the neighbour across the park had let her dog out before she went to bed for the night. The persistent calling for entry back into the dog owner's home had met with no welcoming opened door. The continual barking, for some reason, was not heard by the dog's owner, who was the closest to its source.

A kind and easy-going man—even the most sensitive animal lover—can eventually reach the point of saturation. Ray had tried closing his windows and putting his head under the pillow. He had tried extra drinks and earplugs. Nothing worked for my friend to keep at bay the grinding, cursed sounds: *arf arf, woof, woof.* How can any creature keep barking for so many hours at a time? How can the dog's owner ignore the penetrating, blasphemous cacophony?

This was my first night's loss of sleep. I was tired when I returned from up north, and my hope for a refreshing rest had been interrupted by the sound of barking. From Ray, I had learned that the dog being let out at night was a recent happening. It was the fifth night in a row that Ray had his sleep ruined. I was sitting enjoying an early sunrise, having a cup of tea, watching the morning news broadcast on television, when suddenly I heard the sound of my friend slamming his front door. I peered through the sheers covering the window. I could see Ray marching across his front lawn, he looked angry and I could hear him calling for some quiet.

"I'll kill the bastard," he shouted.

Ray was dressed in a pair of shorts and a thick sweater stretched tight across his enormous belly. He was a very big man in his mid-seventies. A nice and gentle man, despite his military background. He wore a toque and slippers. As he crossed the lawn I could hear him shout to Tom, another long-suffering neighbour.

"Tom, hey Tom, are you there? That blasted dog, I've had enough. Have you got your gun? I'll shoot the bastard," he shouted.

There was silence for a minute or two.

"Thanks Tom, is it loaded? With ten shells you say? That should do it. Now I can get some peace and quiet."

The entire conversation was expressed at high volume, and was intended to be overheard by the owner of the dog.

A strident scream of an upset older lady rang through the air.

"Don't you dare come over here and hurt my dog, he's done nothing wrong. Dogs bark. It's only natural."

Getting into the spirit of things Ray called out, "I'll be right over, don't take the dog into the house now, it's too late for that, I'll go in after him. I'll get the bastard."

The voice came back, "I know who you are now, you're Ray Barnett and I've called the police. They will be here in a minute and they'll stop you from hurting Bruno."

With that, we heard a police cruiser squealing his wheels round the corner and come skidding to a halt in front of the driveway. A young, muscular policeman jumped out of the squad car. He was drawing his revolver as he called out, "You, drop your gun and raise your arms, you're under arrest."

Tom did not have a gun to lend Ray. The gun talk had been a ruse and meant to scare the dog owner. As far as the officer was concerned, though, a gun had been part of the transaction and he had no intention of getting hurt. Threats of armed violence had been made and this was a crime, even in St. Petersburg, Florida.

"Lie on the ground with your hands behind your back," demanded the policeman.

Ray is a heavy man, a retired military officer and engineer. He had heard the policeman in total disbelief, and he didn't move. As it seemed to the cop that he was resisting arrest, he called on his radio for backup. In less than two minutes, another squad car hurtled onto the scene. All the while I was watching this drama unfold, right in our front yard.

The second officer joined his colleague and together they tried to subdue our friend. Ray weighed maybe two hundred and fifty pounds with legs like tree-trunks. He just stood there passively resisting and the two young cops were unable to throw him to the ground. He didn't fight back, he just stood there rigid and refused to fall. After a few minutes, in desperation, the first cop called for further backup and within a couple of moments a third cruiser with a sergeant and a constable squealed onto the scene. Between them, they were able to cart my friend off to jail. For some strange reason, the dog had ceased barking and in a few minutes the dust had settled and the neighbourhood assumed its usual Sunday morning tranquility.

We spent an uneasy morning. Tom came over from next door and suggested we go down to the police station and come to Ray's aid. Really, what could we do? Everyone in our area—with the exception of Bruno's mummy—felt sorry for dear old Ray. He was always so generous with his citrus and bananas. Kids making a shortcut through his yard were never reported; a growl and a yell would scare them off for a while. There didn't seem to be any justice remaining in this world. At seventy-five years old, Ray had been taken away by four policemen for shouting at the old biddy's dog to stop it from barking. Of course, the police having a complaint from a citizen that a neighbor had threatened her dog with a weapon, were obliged to take action and that they did. The only thing we could do for Ray was to have some cash ready in case he might need bail money.

It was around two in the afternoon when a chastened Ray was driven to his house in a cab. He quietly entered his little bungalow and shut the door. He remained unseen for most of the day. It seemed a bit odd in a way, because it was a glorious, sunny, afternoon. The kind of day that drew most folks outdoors to the beach or for other fun, outdoor activities. Florida is all about having fun on the beach. On this particular Sunday, Ray did not feel up to his usual self. While I was gathering some grapefruit from our garden, I did see him in his yard for a few minutes while he was picking some tomatoes for supper. I waved to him and he acknowledged my greeting, but did not want to chat.

The next day, Monday, he was up early and waiting outside for a cab. I had never seen Ray dressed like that: blazer, white shirt and a tie, grey slacks and shiny, black shoes. At first I wondered who it was. I was up and about and stepped out of the front door.

"Good morning Ray," I called out. "Have you got time for a coffee?"

"Later Trev," he replied. "Right now I've got to see a man about a dog." A taxi arrived and whisked him away.

Well, it was late that afternoon when Ray came over to our place for coffee. He looked like his old self in his shorts, T-shirt and sandals. We sat in the living room out of the hot sun drinking our coffee while I encouraged Ray to tell us what happened that morning.

"You see, I was told to be at the magistrate's office at nine this morning," he said matter-of-factly. "It's always a good idea to dress properly for that type of meeting." He took a long drink from his coffee and settled back in his chair.

"I had to answer to a charge of threatening bodily harm with a weapon. There were other charges too, such as resisting arrest and disturbing the peace. Hell Trev, I'm seventy-five years old, I am a law-abiding citizen and a proud American veteran with medals to prove it. I don't owe a dime in this world. There was no gun, and there never was. I then explained to the magistrate that it was the blasted dog who was disturbing the peace, not me. We chatted a while about a number of things and it turned out that he didn't like barking dogs either. He gave me a warning to keep the peace, and that was that."

It was after five o'clock and the sun was beginning to cool down.

Time to invite our neighbor Tom to join us and crack open a fresh bottle of vodka. The three of us sat and watched the sun go down as we enjoyed our drinks. We used our own fresh-squeezed limes and as we mellowed out, we began to see aspects of the case which caused us some merriment. Especially the part about it taking four young, strong men, St. Petersburg's finest, to arrest our elderly pal.

Note: This excerpt is from Trevor C. Trower's book, titled Phyllis The Donkey Girl and Other True Tales. *It was published by Tamarind Tree Books in 2020.*

TREVOR C. TROWER

Trevor C. Trower was born in England. Prior to emigrating, in 1952 he was a photographer with British Empire Films. After 35 years with Air Canada In-Flight service, Trevor retired and pursued hobbies such as model trains and archaeology. His latest collection is *Phyllis The Donkey Girl* (Tamarind Tree Books, 2020). Trevor lives in Georgetown, Ontario, with his wife of 64 years, Kay Thompson.

MARY ELLEN KOROSCIL

Road Apples on Chestnut Avenue

Let's take time out from the world-weary pandemic that has raged on. Put on a happy face and escape with me to the good ole days of the Forties and Fifties for a Moose Jaw, Saskatchewan style adventure. If you haven't been there, then you haven't really lived!

Through my childhood eyes, I will take you back to 1946. I was just a year old. My family and I lived in a two-room, upstairs suite in my grandparent's home. Living in cramped quarters was worth it, as Mom and Dad were saving to buy a house. Nobody had any money in those days, but everyone was in the same pickle. We had a second-storey veranda that featured windows on all sides. It was nice 'n airy in the summer. I've seen pictures of me, out in the porch and perched in my high chair, basking in the warm sunshine.

However, the winter was a different story. That veranda was freezing cold and drafty.

"You could build a snowman in there," my mother admitted to me. "Your Dad and I were scared that you would freeze to death in your crib before you were two."

My Mom's name was Lois and Dad was Malcolm, or Mac for short. They finally did save enough cash for a down payment on a $3,500 home on Chestnut Avenue. We moved from Second Ave. N.E. to Chestnut Avenue, one whole street over. Our new place was a big, ole, three-storey home. Nowadays we would call it a "handyman special," but we didn't care, this was our very own house.

Most mornings we could hear the clip-clop of a chestnut mare's hooves as the horse laboured, pulling the Palm Dairy milk wagon up our hilly street. On a good day we were even allowed to pet the horse. We understood, of course, that our avenue was named after the horse.

Years later, my own kids looked at me in disbelief when I told them about our home, and said: "Mom, you really lived in pioneer times with a horse-drawn milk wagon."

Back in those warm summers the milk was kept cold with ice, and on a hot day the milkman would hand out ice chips to us children to keep us cool. In the winter, the dairy didn't need ice, as it would be about thirty-five to forty degrees below for about four months.

One thing that did freeze nicely and that slid out of the horse's behind, was its lumps of manure. These were known as "road apples." The hockey players on the street used them as pucks and missed them when the dairy became modernized. Few parents could afford real pucks. You wouldn't dare bring these road apples inside the house, because they would thaw. Around 1949 or 1950, the horses were put out to pasture and Palm Dairy amassed a fleet of milk trucks. These streamlined trucks sported a palm tree logo emblazed on the side of the vehicle. In the midst of a stinging blizzard, the palm tree logo would appear like an oasis on the frozen horizon of the rough-and-tumble prairies.

Winter seemed never-ending. For fun, we went sleigh riding and tobogganing at Shabbits Hill around the corner. All the kids were there. Then a doctor built a modern house on that hilly, vacant lot. (Why would he want to do that?) We were out of luck.

That left us with skating on the outdoor rink, by Ross School. By the age of three most kids had been on skates, by four they were whizzing along the ice. At the age of five, we thought we were Olympic material. To keep the skaters from getting frost bite, the city placed a nice-sized shack near the rink. They hired Sam as a shack supervisor. It was his job to maintain the peace and to keep the wood-burning potbelly stove filled. He was a big, friendly, rotund fellow with a pronounced limp.

After skating for half an hour I could feel my five-year-old face tingling, which meant it was time to hit the shack. The first thing that greeted you upon entering was the wonderful stove, nestled in the corner, spitting out heat. One time, my Dad and I were warming ourselves and Sam was talking to this rather scruffy-looking kid of about ten who carved a piece of wood with a jack knife. There were shavings all over the floor.

Sam, in a booming voice said: "Kid, you better clean up your mess, and do it now," as he threw the broom and dustpan on the bench. The boy didn't move, and Sam reiterated. "Get to it."

Much to our horror, with a flick of his wrist the boy threw his knife and it landed in Sam's leg. Dad grabbed hold of me and pulled me toward the door. Just then we heard Sam roar with laughter. We saw him pull the knife out of his leg. He wasn't in pain and there was no blood.

He yelled: "I'll keep your knife as a souvenir. Now get the hell out of here, or I'll call the cops, you're damn lucky." He rolled up his pant leg to show off his hand-made wooden leg. Years later I learned that for entertainment value this was an amazing performance that Sam and this kid acted out many times to unsuspecting skaters. Only in Moose Jaw!

My parents were kept busy fixing up the house. In order to pay for renovations we rented out the second floor. Miss Shoji lived in the front two-room suite. She was a fitness instructor at the "Y." She was from Germany, spoke with a heavy accent and she was in topnotch shape. Not an extra pound on her slender frame. However, she was a bit of a health nut.

She refused to have curtains on the two front windows, saying: "I want the natural light. Forget about drapes."

We weren't sure if she waltzed around naked, in full view of the neighbours. Miss Shoji kept apples (real ones) in the icebox and she would roll them in the dirt, in the backyard before eating them—she would simply whisk them off a little, as she believed "a little dirt never hurt anyone."

The other two upstairs rooms were occupied by the Wilsons, a lively, white haired couple in their sixties, who were farmers. They worked the land for half a year in Briercrest, and lived with us for the other six months.

I recall a staircase in the main upstairs hall leading to my special place, the attic. One of the unfinished rooms had a big window and a regular, finished floor. The largest room at the front only had a partial floor. Every second board in the row was missing, and my dad told me: "If you step off the boards you will go crashing through the ceiling into Miss Shoji's suite." I was very careful to pick and choose where I walked. Surprisingly enough, my

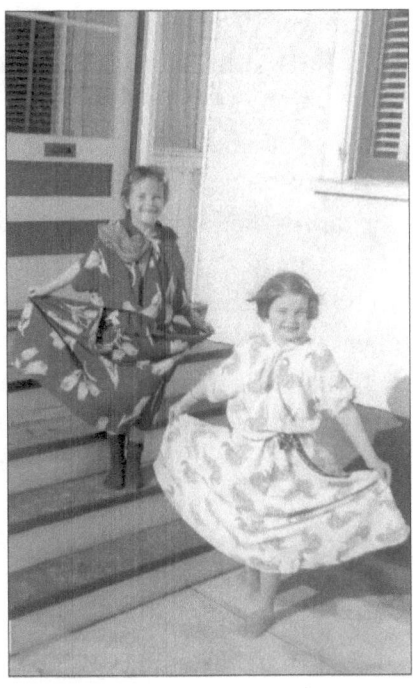

Pictured – 1953 posing on the front steps of Muriel's house, on First Avenue N.E., Moose Jaw, Sask., Mary Ellen McBride on the left and Muriel Grainger on the right, modelling Muriel's mother's dresses.

five-year-old body never bolted down through the ceiling. I was saved from having to eat "dirty apples" with Miss Shoji.

A real treat for me was when my mom would take my friend Muriel and me to Crescent Park. We would take bread crusts to feed the swans and then have a picnic with Mom's egg salad sandwiches. There was also a wonderful kids' play area in the park with swings, monkey bars and a neat wading pool.

One summer, however, my mom said, "We can't let you kids in the pool or use the swings or monkey bars as you might end up contracting polio."

No kids were allowed in the play area, if I recall correctly, until we were all vaccinated, and then we could resume playing on the bars. Reminds me of what is currently happening in our world today. History does repeat itself. I do recall at school seeing some kids on crutches who had contracted polio; it was a terrible disease.

Crescent Park, in "The Jaw," is still a beautiful spot today and the swans still swim in the creek. My close friend Linda Rae is lucky enough to live in a condo opposite that lush and lovely park. It sort of reminds me of High Park in Toronto.

A few houses up the block was where my friend Sandy lived. Her family had a big house with three verandas. Our favourite one was a sort of dark and spooky back porch. It was enclosed and we would place blankets over our heads and run around scaring each other.

In Sandy's living room there was a cabinet-style record player. LPs were piled up and came down, one by one, automatically. My favourites were the Walt Disney ones. They had corresponding story books, featuring Tweety and Sylvester titled *I Thout I saw a Puddy Cat*. That was Tweety's famous last words. Another favourite was the antics of Donald Duck, and Goofy. We played those storybook records over and over again.

Luckily, I now had a new playmate at home. He was my baby brother Rob, "who had a round face like Winston Churchill's" my Mom used to say. I liked holding him, but ever so carefully and watching him try to wave his arms and smile. And I wanted him to grow up quickly so we could be best pals. But I knew it would be some time before he could walk around and learn to play.

So, in the meantime, waiting for my brother to grow up I had to chum around with my neighbourhood friends. I'd stroll up the back alley to Muriel's house. Today we would hang out in her back porch where there was a long shutter that opened and closed. It was for hanging out clothes on the washing line. We opened and closed the shutter, would stick our heads out and make strange sounds, just like in the movies. Then we would play spy with clothes pins, sending secret notes along the line to each other.

It didn't take much to entertain Muriel and I. For hours, we played bumping down the long staircase from the second storey. We sat beside each other, having a race to reach the bottom, without a pillow underneath us. And speaking about bottoms, mine would be aching and awfully sore when I left her house. I couldn't figure out why we did that?

Another Chestnut Avenue friend was Judy. Her mom gave us cones of delicious chocolate ice cream. With dripping cones in hand, we strolled up the block to our friend Beryl's home.

Beryl had a neat bedroom, I believe her dad had built, at the end of the living room. In it was a metal bunk bed. Apparently her dad bought it from the army surplus barracks, after the war. We used to do tricks swinging on the top bunk down to the bottom. Beryl was a gymnast, she was double jointed, she could twist and turn like a trapeze artist. She took gym lessons at the "Y." Every year during a "Y" show we would be there watching our friend, The Star.

In her family's kitchen they had a secret basement. It looked like an ordinary, linoleum floor, but you could pull the latch that lifted up, and attach it to the wall. Lo and behold, stairs appeared leading down. And when you came back up, Beryl's mom would close the floor up again, just like magic!

Chestnut Avenue was filled with entrepreneurs, though they were never called that during the Fifties, they were just folks earning a living.

Across the street was the furrier, they were the Halls. My mom took me there when she was fitted for a mouton coat. She told me: "Mouton is the cheapest fur, less expensive than beaver, which weighs a ton." The Hall's large garage was the furrier shop. There were fluorescent lights, and it smelled like animals' furs. There were two industrial sewing machines and a big cutting table in the middle of the room. Mrs. Hall had made a catalogue with pictures of fur coats that she and her husband designed and sewed, and she showed samples to my mom and me and let us feel the mouton. To this day I don't know which animal would produce a mouton coat. The fur felt so soft and pliable. My mother's coat was jet black, but boy, was it warm. She wore it for a few years. When she left us I found it very hard to part with her treasured fur coat.

Kitty-corner across the street lived the Bull family. They had a home-based photography business. I still have a photo they took of me sitting on a coffee table at about age six with one leg tucked under me, posing for a formal sitting. I would never be able to get out of that pose today, my leg would surely seize right up. I was wearing a blue taffeta dress that my mom made for me. My beautiful mother was a real sewing whiz and all-round talented woman. When making a pie, she could peel an apple with a paring knife in two swoops. She wrote poetry too, and submitted her poems to the *Moose Jaw Times Herald*. I wish I could recall if they were ever published. I remember and appreciate my dad too, he was such a hard worker. He was a printer, and would arrive home all "round-shouldered," as my mother would say, from bending over a printing press all day. After supper he would tackle house renovations. Things were rosier when he landed a better-paying office job, working for the City.

Directly across the street lived a couple and I can't remember their last name. They didn't have any children, but they had a dandy collection of dentures instead. He was a denturist. In the living room were wall shelves containing curious samples of dentures that he had made, complete with bright, pink gums. Some of the dentures contained mighty big teeth. In the day, we used to call them buckteeth. When you met a senior on Main Street you could see them coming for miles, when they grinned, bearing those giant teeth. To think that they were made right across the street from me. I believe this is where my grandfather bought his dentures. However, they must have been on a clearance sale, for they developed a hole in them. When he spoke spit would ease through the gaping hole. When we were invited over to visit this couple I couldn't take my eyes off the dentures; however, I hoped that I would never have the pleasure of wearing such big "choppers."

Chestnut Avenue was the best place on earth for me and my little brother. Too bad we had to move suddenly, but I'll save that tale for another time.

MARY ELLEN KOROSCIL

Mary Ellen Koroscil operates a public-relations business, M.E.K. Specialty Services Inc., working with authors, editing manuscripts and assisting in book promotion. She also writes poetry and short stories and is the Chair of Courtney Park Writers, a group of inspirational, mutually supportive authors and poets.

KUMKUM RAMCHANDANI

A Pandemic Problem

To: Raj@coronav.in
9:00 a.m.
21 March, 2020

Hello Jaanu:

We are missing you so much! Who knew this would happen? Amit and Amrita are constantly asking when will Papa come back to Dubai? They are like parrots. It's driving me crazy. I have no answer except to wait for this stupid virus to be over. Wish you hadn't listened to Mummyji. You know she's a hypochondriac. When she said her back was broken, you went running to Delhi to look after her, even though she has Babu Ram and Lalita to attend to her twenty-four-seven.

After all, we're paying both of them 40,000 rupees monthly. And they are growing fat digging into the basmati rice and ghee, as Mummyji doesn't lock anything up. Plus, all the fruit and vegetables that arrive weekly from that crazily expensive shop in Khan Market. You know, last October when I was there, the cost of each grapefruit was 100 rupees. Daylight robbery, I tell you. Just because all the Europeans and diplomats flock to their shops, they feel free to overcharge the rest of us!

Now you're stuck there and god knows when the airlines will start flying again ... please install Zoom so we can chat. However, please talk to us when Mummyji is not around, otherwise she'll monopolize the conversation. I'm not being mean; you too said she talks too much. I have to go now, as A and A are asking for a pancake breakfast. I hope they don't come out hard and chewy like last time.

Gosh, I really miss Chote Lal, wish he hadn't gone on vacation because now he's stuck too. He cannot leave his village. He called and said the buses from the village to Lucknow are under lockdown. He can't get back in the near future. I now realize what a boon he is, as I'm going nuts cooking and cleaning. The kitchen is a mess. The kids are cooped up and bored. They're going to start online classes, as the schools close next week. Another headache for me ... sigh! Missing you, Jaanu.

Love,

Sangeeta

To: Sang@gmail.ae
10:00 p.m.
22 March, 2020

Hi Darling,

Don't worry, this coronavirus will blow over. Delhi is in total lockdown. So is Dubai. A former US president says it's "a storm in a teacup." He believes all developed countries have the means to combat anything. I was in touch with the office and they agreed that I can work online, so I have already installed Zoom. My working hours will remain the same. I took Mummyji to the spinal hospital today. They took X-rays. If they can't find anything, they will have to do an MRI. I'm dreading that. How will she keep still and quiet for 45 minutes?

Anyway, keep your spirits up, things always work out in the end, don't they? Don't get hassled, you know your blood pressure will go up and then you'll feel dizzy. Chin up, dear girl. Lots of love to the brats. I'm tired, and off to bed. Today Babu Ram made sarson ka saag and makki ki roti, it was heavenly! Mummyji seems upbeat, she even had a small scotch and soda with me in the evening!

Anyway, kiss, kiss, will talk again....Your loving hubby.

To: Raj@coronav.in
9:00 a.m.
23 March, 2020

Hello Raj,

Wow, you seem quite cheerful. Aren't you missing us? I was watching BBC—looks like this virus is spreading to Italy and Spain. They're badly hit, with many people dying. Do you think this is nature's way of getting rid of the weak? I know this sounds callous, but I think we humans have been screwing with the planet and this is the revenge.

Anyway, back to our life here. Dubai is sanitizing the streets and we are not allowed out between ten p.m. and six a.m. We must obtain an online permit to enter the store or pharmacy. Everything else is shuttered. Only one person at a time can shop. I have to do everything on my own. A and A are watching a lot of Netflix. Amit plays computer games the rest of the time and Amrita is on the phone with her friends almost twenty-four-seven.

I made pizza last night. It didn't taste as good as Chote Lal's but the kids actually ate some of it. Tonight, they want McDonald's so I will indulge them. Only home delivery is allowed. Lucky you, eating home-cooked meals by Desi Khana. Was the sarson from Mummyji's vegetable garden? Oh god, I have tons of laundry to do. Amit goes through ten T-shirts a day and our princess wants to wear nice clothes, even though there's nowhere to go...

Your wifey.

To: Sang@gmail.ae
8:00 p.m.
25 March, 2020

Hey Wifey,

Sorry, I couldn't be in touch yesterday. It was crazy-busy. I set up my new computer to be in touch with the clients and had to upload tons of information so that I could follow up on their investments. Mummyji's X-rays didn't show any damage, except the osteoporosis, which we know she has. When she heard about what the MRI would entail, she threw a fit. She is refusing to do it and says she is feeling hardly any pain now. She is walking about without her walker.

Yesterday she was in the kitchen making gajar ka halwa. She was actually singing "tu cheez bari hai mast mast." You know how she loves that song. She wants to host a dinner party and invite her bridge group. I told her that it's not a good idea. They are all in the high-risk group, over seventy and mostly with hypertension and diabetes. Hope she doesn't go ahead, you know how she can be quite headstrong! Let's talk on Zoom tomorrow afternoon. Mummyji has her nap after lunch, so say around 2:30 p.m., Delhi time? Hope you're feeling less anxious, my Jaan.

Your loving hubby.

To: Raj@coronav.in
9:00 a.m.
25 March, 2020

What do you mean "quite headstrong?" She is totally a battering ram. I told you nothing is wrong with her, she only wanted to see her darling Beta. Gosh, Raj, when will you learn? She's manipulative, always has been. She never wanted you to marry me. She had her eye on that Sharma girl—the right fit for you, pretty, a great cook and so good-natured ... just a fat cow, in my opinion. Anyway, I have to go now.

The kids' online classes start tomorrow and I have to work with them on their class subjects ... sigh! Thank god we have two computers and I am IT savvy. I bet your fat cow wouldn't have been able to set up online classes ... ha! Let's have a Zoom meeting in the afternoon ...

Sangeeta.

To: Sang@gmail.ae
8:00 p.m.
26 March, 2020

Sorry you have to deal with all this on your own, Sangeeta, but who could foresee this? I will be back as soon as I can. As for Mummyji, she is my mother after all. She is alone in this world, except for me. I have to look after her. I'm sorry she stayed awake yesterday afternoon. She told me she really enjoyed talking to you all on Zoom. I think it really helped her health to chat with her grandchildren. She told me later that god knows when she will see them again. Who knows what happens in one's life, it's all in the hands of the Almighty.

Please give an old lady her due respect. She adores Amit and Amrita. I know you have your differences, but please be understanding, Sangeeta.

As for Renu Sharma, she was never a consideration. I never looked upon her as marriage material. How can you forget that when I saw you, it was like lightning had struck me. I repeat, for the umpteenth time, I love your dusky skin, I love your fiery temper, your intelligence and the fact that you are not only my partner in marriage, but, also someone with whom I can discuss anything under the sun.

Raj.

To: Raj@coronav.in
8:00 p.m.
27 March, 2020

I'm sorry, Raj, I think this virus is getting under my skin. I've cut short my time on WhatsApp and Facebook and only watch the BBC News at night. It's all too depressing. The kids and I are missing meeting our friends. Even when I call up somebody we invariably end up discussing the situation. There are so many conspiracy theories floating around, one doesn't know what to believe.

Also, the brats are fighting more than usual. Yesterday Amit was using the hair dryer when his sister wanted it. He took his own sweet time because he knew she wanted it. It escalated into a humongous battle with both of them calling each other horrible names.

Then I started crying and the tears just wouldn't stop. They were so startled that they forgot their fight and came to hug me. Then all of us cried. Seems so funny now, it wasn't then, believe me.

Sangeeta.

To: Sang@gmail.ae
10:00 p.m.
28 March, 2020

I can just imagine all of you crying ... how sad, but funny too. I have tears in my eyes, I am missing you so much now. Yesterday, I was really mean to Mummyji. She can't seem to understand that I cannot be disturbed, during my working hours. She keeps walking into the bedroom where I do my office work, to ask me what I want to eat, not just for lunch and dinner, but even for the next day. I think I'm putting on weight. I miss your cooking even though you burn it sometimes or add too much salt (it's a joke my love).

At least I don't pig out at home, like I'm doing here. Also, she keeps talking about old times and mentioning people I have no clue about. I just cut out, but then the next day she repeats the same old stuff ... grrrr.

Sang, will we get so irritating when we grow old? Let's not be that way. If we make up our minds to always be interesting and with it, I'm sure we will not end up like her. I'm dying to get back to Dubai; however, I guess I have to grin and bear it until the flights open up again. On a positive note: Delhi is tackling the coronavirus with great success.

Raj.

To: Raj@coronav.ae
9:00 a.m.
30 March, 2020

Guess what? I opened up my oil paints box last night and discovered an old photo that I've been wanting to paint forever. Remember that Masai warrior you photographed ten years ago when we went to Kenya? I have started sketching and doing preliminary rough transfers. And I went on YouTube and saved a cookery tutorial on Mexican dishes. I made quesadillas for dinner and the kids polished everything off. What a wonderful feeling. I guess by the time you get back, I will be an artist once again and will be able to make your favourite dishes! It's so easy when you have YouTube in front of you.

Must go, the brats start their online lessons today. I'll have to be around until they're settled into a routine. They should be done by three p.m., then we'll have lunch and I will get back to my painting ... you take care, Jaanu. Don't worry, we're fine, we will get over this damn thing together, even if we are apart. Give my love to Mummyji.

Your loving wifey,
Sang.

To: Sang@gmail.ae
9:00 a.m.
31 March, 2020

Hello my darling,

Mummyji was very pleased that you had sent her your love. She said about a hundred times not to forget to send love back to you. She also said that once this virus-shirus is over she wouldn't mind coming to visit us for a few months. She said Mrs. Khanna went all the way to Australia, to visit her family. It was a comfortable flight because her son paid for a business class ticket and she had a wheelchair and an attendant all to herself.

Don't cringe, Jaanu, it's not going to happen, you know she hates to be outside her comfort zone. How many times has she said she was coming to Dubai and then cancelled at the last minute!

I'm missing you guys a lot but am busy with work, which helps to pass the time. I think you're right about Mummyji being manipulative. I told her that I'm leaving as soon as the flights resume and sure enough she started complaining about her back pain! I guess from now on I have to learn to put my foot down.

You know what, this coronavirus has made me think ... we should change our priorities. I don't think I really need a new car. We're lucky to have everything we need, but what's more important? For me, it's you and the kids ... I wish to spend time doing fun stuff again, with all of you. Beach trips, swimming, camping: the things we never seem to have time for. Basically, stop and smell the roses! And if Mummyji is part of this, so be it ... (just kidding!) Glad to know that you are painting and cooking. I can't wait to be with you all.

Hugs and kisses,
Raj.

KUMKUM RAMCHANDANI

Kumkum Ramchandani was raised in India, lived in the United Arab Emirates, Nigeria, Canada and now resides in Dubai. Her book of short stories entitled *Dadiji & Other Stories* was published in 2020. She is a writer and an artist. View her artwork, including mosaics, on Facebook under Kumkum's Artwork.

KEN MARVELL

Everyday Happenings

Not Another Line-Up At The Bank...

Years ago when the bank I frequented was located in the old Milton Mall, it was always extremely busy on Thursday and Friday evenings, especially on the fifteenth and thirtieth of each month. These were paydays for many people and online banking was not as yet a common option.

Thinking back, I am sure that between staff and customers, there were many nights when the bank was over the legal capacity allowed for the number of people in a public space.

One Friday evening I found myself standing in an awfully long queue that ran from the bank's entrance doors all the way up to about three or four feet near the tellers' wickets, at which point customers would advance to the "Next Available Teller." Between the start and end of the queue, the bank's crowd control consisted of rope barriers in a zigzag formation back and forth, in order to handle more customers and to ensure no one jumped ahead of the others.

After shuffling forward all of about twenty feet in the stuffy, over-crowded bank, I had plenty of time to observe many bank employees who were looking ever so busy and important. They scurried back and forth from desk to desk, doing who-knows-what. In the meantime, the bank had six or eight teller wickets; however, only four of them were open to serve the never-ending line of customers.

If watching this unfold wasn't frustrating enough, I happened to notice an 8" x 12" poster taped high up near the ceiling on a post, so as to be visible to every customer. It was a photograph of all the bank employees with smiling faces. Across the picture was a comment in bold print that read: "Waiting To Serve You." Immediately, a thought entered my mind and I commented out loud. "Someone should take a picture of all of us customers crammed in together like sardines, and post it under their poster. Then in bold letters, write across it, "Waiting To Be Served By You."

Many of the frustrated customers standing nearby broke out in laughter when they heard my comment and soon voiced their agreement.

A Coffee Shop Encounter...

I walked into the coffee shop and immediately found myself in a line of eight or nine customers, waiting to be served. The line moved at a snail's pace. One employee was taking the customers' orders and punching them into the cash register, then dealing with the cash transactions, while another employee poured the coffees for that order. So, the line should have moved quickly. However, that first employee then went to retrieve the donuts or scones for the customers. A few other employees were busy making sandwiches and refilling the donut trays in the display cases.

Looking over at the drive-thru window, there were at least five employees taking and filling orders. Observing how fast that line of cars was being served, I even considered walking out of the store, getting back into my car, and heading to the drive-thru myself to order my beverage. Then, once I received my coffee, I would park my car and walk back into the coffee shop, sit at a table, and take my time to enjoy my cup of coffee. That would have been a solution rather than standing for ages in the line-up.

However, I didn't think of doing that soon enough. Eventually I struck up a conversation with a gentleman who was standing behind me and I jokingly said, "The service is so slow, perhaps they are being trained by the banks."

He and a few others standing nearby overheard me, and we all had a laugh. It's good to see the funny side of things.

Local Coffee Shop And Chelios

One evening as I was about to enter a local coffee shop, a man who looked to be in his early thirties waited and held the door open for me, to catch up to him. I said, "Thank you!"

Once inside, we were the only two customers in line.

"You go ahead of me," he said. "I haven't decided what I want to order."

Again I said, "Thank you!"

Then touching the brim of my Detroit Red Wings hockey cap and pointing to the Wings' logo, I asked jokingly if the cap was the reason I was getting so much respect.

He looked at my Red Wings Cap and replied, "Oh, I thought you were Chris Chelios, the Red Wings defenseman."

After a short pause, I looked him in the eye and said, "Is that meant to be a compliment to me or an insult to Chris Chelios?"

We both chuckled. Come to think of it, he never did reply.

The Bank Teller...

As was my custom back in the day, I went to my local bank to pay bills and withdraw some money.

Talking with the teller, a pleasant lady who was handling my transactions, our conversation went something like this.

"I don't recall seeing you here before," I said.

She replied, "I have been here a few times, actually, I have worked for the bank for over twenty years."

"Well, it's a pleasure meeting you."

The teller processed the payment of my bills, walked over to the back counter and stamped them, showing they were paid and the date of payment. I mention this because the bank was trying to end this practice of stamping the bills as being paid. God only knows why?

She walked back to her wicket and asked me, "How much do you want to withdraw?"

"$200 please."

"What denominations would you like?"

To which I replied, as I tried to keep a serious expression on my face: "Three Anglicans, two Roman Catholics, and the balance in Baptists would be just fine."

Instantly her face flushed beet red as she burst out laughing and said, "Twenty years in the banking business and I have never heard that one before."

I said, "It's an old one, going way back to the days of Jack Benny. Most people would be too embarrassed to tell it but, at my age, I'm not. Besides, it put a smile on your face and gave you a laugh."

Still smiling, she replied, "It sure did that. Thank you, you made my day."

More Brewing Than Coffee...

A few years ago while in Oakville, I went into the coffee shop located on Bronte Road, south of the Queen Elizabeth Way.

It was a dark, stormy night. The high blustery winds were whipping heavy raindrops against the large panes of glass. It sounded so bad outside that the customers were in no rush to leave.

As I stood in line, there were two couples, both in their mid-to-late-twenties ahead of me. In spite of the fact that there were a dozen or more people sitting at tables sipping their drinks, one of the couples started becoming amorous by hugging and kissing.

As the service seemed to be slow for some reason, the couple's actions became hot and heavy while they stood there in the line. Some people, noticing them, started feeling uncomfortable and commented out loud, "Get a room" or "Take it home."

The couple seemed to take their comments as encouragement and just smiled. They continued sucking tongues as their two bodies became as one.

It was only after I quietly made a comment to them, that they immediately stopped and burst into laughter. What I said was: "Why don't you just knock it off? There are married people in here and it's not fair to them."

The Mask...

Recently I went to the pharmacy to pick up a prescription.

Before entering I put on my COVID-19 mask and made sure it

was securely in place. Once inside, I stood on one of the designated COVID spacing marks painted on the floor. (For future readers, those markings were placed there as a guide so that people standing in line would keep their distance and not risk spreading the virus.)

There was a woman standing ahead of me picking up her prescription. After paying, the woman turned to leave and I realized I knew her, so I said: "Hi!"

She greeted me in turn with a "Hi!"

I followed up with: "How are you?"

Walking away she coolly replied, "Fine!"

The pleasant cashier and I looked at each other, both taken aback by the woman's abruptness. I indicated, "I've known her for years. Our kids even attended school together and went to one another's birthday parties." Then, patting my mask with both hands, jokingly I said to the young lady, "I guess she didn't recognise me with clothes on!"

The cashier burst out laughing. Then, after a few moments allowing her to compose herself I told her, "If you liked my joke that much, you can use it."

Still laughing she replied, "That was so funny!" I'll be sure to tell it to the pharmacists."

KEN MARVELL

Born in Montreal in the 1940s, Ken Marvell was raised in St. Paul L'Ermite, a predominantly French-speaking village. Since 2012 he's written memoirs and true stories: mostly humorous in nature with the exception of some paranormal. His memoirs are published in five anthologies and in a magazine. He resides in Milton, Ontario.

ZOHRA ZOBERI

The Mystery of Malisa

Blessed with a figure like Sophia Loren, how could she go un-noticed? Her silky red hair fell well below her shoulders and bounced as she walked. Her light, European complexion and lovely facial features didn't represent any typical origin. So she could pass as French, Spanish, Italian, or from just about anywhere in the Middle East.

Once she had settled herself in the chair across from my desk at the bank, and the introductions were completed, I asked: "How much are you depositing in your account?"

"Five hundred," she whispered.

"And how much would you like to withdraw?"

"Five hundred," she replied again softly.

"You are depositing five hundred … but also withdrawing five hundred?"

"I'm depositing five hundred thousand, withdrawing only five hundred dollars."

She handed me a bank draft—five hundred thousand dollars.

I gasped as I glanced at the information sheet, which confirmed that she was only twenty-four years old. By the time I finished completing the transaction and her transfers of funds from other banks, the total amount came to almost two million dollars. This was definitely a God-sent gift for me as we were in the middle of an aggressive campaign for bringing in new money to our bank branch. Her name, Malisa Khan, raised my curiosity.

"Miss Khan, may I ask where you are from?"

"Niagara Falls."

"Niagara Falls? I … I mean…" She sensed my hesitation.

"Oh, you mean originally. I'm a Parsee from Iranian background, married to a Pathan from the Frontier."

She must have guessed my background and assumed that I would understand her reference to *The Frontier. They had just moved to Toronto from Niagara Falls where they had sold a hotel they owned, which explained the hefty deposit that so delighted me.

Once the transactions were finalized, we chatted for a few minutes. I mentioned to her that across the street from our new home was a four-bedroom, luxury house that overlooked a ravine...and it was for sale. The next day she and her husband Rehmat Khan came to view the property, made an on-the-spot offer for which they paid in full, and became my neighbours. They were probably the only mortgage-free couple in that affluent locale.

Soon we were on the list of their favourite guests. Mr. Khan loved to barbeque and we enjoyed socializing with them and their friends. Malisa was a brilliant young woman, educated in a convent school in Goa. Rehmat worked at a butcher shop in Mississauga. Since butchering may be considered more working class in some communities, they were a very unusual match from the Indo-Pakistani, cultural perspective. However, I found them interesting and mysterious. In the entranceway of their new home, a huge marble pedestal supported an impressive, original bronze sculpture by a well-known French artist. Yet they cooked food in dented and stained pots and served it in the crudest manner I had ever witnessed.

Once, my husband and I accepted an invitation to join them at a downtown nightclub called The Heaven. That evening, on the dance floor, it seemed as if most of the young guys were finding themselves in *heaven*, dancing with their girlfriends while ogling Malisa as she wiggled on by.

"Some of the guys would have experienced strained necks by the end of the evening," I remarked to my hubby.

Malisa was fashionably dressed in a turquoise, silk, one-piece jump suit with a plunging neckline that exposed her well-endowed bosom. As she gyrated erotically to Chubby Checkers' "The Twist" it was evident that beneath the flimsy silk, she wore no undergarments.

"I believe 'The Twist' was instantly chosen by the DJ who spotted her." I whispered to my husband.

He sarcastically replied, "I can understand why he's staring at her, but why are you staring at her?"

"It's hard to look away. You don't seem able to do it either."

In contrast to her exotic appearance, her husband was dressed ever so sloppily.

I had once asked Malisa: "Your husband seems kind of conservative, doesn't he object to the way you dress?"

She replied: "Please … please Shamaila, don't ever bring it up in front of him. This is the only area where I get to exercise complete freedom."

One night they asked us to join them at their home for after-dinner tea and dessert. When we arrived, I was shocked and embarrassed to see that she was in her lingerie! Black, see-through, chiffon harem pants with side slits up to the top of her thigh. My husband could hardly keep his eyes off of her.

Can I blame him? I thought to myself.

On the way home, I criticized Malisa's revealing lingerie, which my hubby readily defended: "It shows they feel comfortable with us."

After a rather unpleasant exchange, he announced: "Anyway, it's none of our business how she was dressed."

"Or undressed," I added.

A few months later, Rehmat travelled out of the country for a three-month business trip, which meant that Malisa was left behind with their two little kids. It was during this time that she and I became closer. She was a lonely neighbour in need of company. Since she couldn't leave her small children alone at night, I went to her house. We watched sappy movies, shed tears and shared emotional stories of our childhoods; all of which seemed to bond us.

A few months later, she made a trip abroad and brought back some semi-precious jewellery to sell. I didn't fancy anything much, except for a pair of black jade earrings set in pewter. So when I expressed my interest, she held them against her heart: "Sorry Shamaila, but these aren't for sale as they have a deep sentimental value for me." Malisa didn't seem eager to share the details of the sentiment, so I didn't press the issue.

One day we were invited for a dinner gathering at her place. I was almost finished dressing when I received a call from Malisa who sounded stranger than usual. "Please don't come over this evening. Rehmat is upset over how close my friendship with you has become and that's something he cannot tolerate. I can't talk right now. I have to go. Bye."

I put down the receiver in disbelief. Days and months passed when we hardly saw the couple. I wondered how Malisa could be so cold ... how Rehmat could be so controlling.

After a few months, much to my surprise and relief, Malisa showed up at the bank, profusely apologizing for her strange behaviour. "Please don't take it personally Shamaila. You are not the first close friendship my husband made me end."

"Made you?" was all I could utter. By then I was angry with both of them, Rehmat for being so controlling and Malisa for being so submissive.

After that encounter at my workplace, Malisa mysteriously disappeared once again; until one Saturday morning she caught me by surprise, when she dropped in unannounced at my home. She was dressed in a black leather mini-skirt, fishnet stockings, and a plunging neck-line. The sight was a challenge to my inferiority complex. Perhaps even Sophia Loren might have felt a twinge of envy.

"I just wanted to tell you we've sold the house and we are leaving the country, for good. Rehmat left yesterday. I'm following with the children tonight."

She said it as casually as if saying she'd just picked up the dry cleaning. I was once again dumbfounded.

Strange as she appeared to be, I still invited her in. She barely crossed the entrance hallway threshold. She seemed to need to remain close to the door. "I can't stay. I've only come to say good bye."

I was struggling with what to say. *I'm sorry you're leaving? Or else: It makes no difference since we don't see each other anyway?*

"Oh really?" was all I could offer.

I turned to see my husband approaching. He seemed anxious to have one last look ... and he took a rather long one at that. Then in a flash she was gone. In a jumble of nerves and confusion, I began to chatter away to my husband. "Did you see how she was dressed? Who dresses like that for a long flight with two small children? Don't you think she kind of looked like a hooker?"

"Not at all," he quickly replied. "She's just very modern, that's all. I didn't see anything wrong with her outfit."

"Okay darling, next time I fly across the globe I'll dress like that. Then we'll see if you find anything wrong with it."

He smiled and embraced me, "Ah! My dear, why wait? If you would dress like that for me tonight, I'd love it."

I wasn't in the mood for a joke because, silly or not, I felt sad that this time, Malisa had left for good.

As I locked the front door, I noticed a small paper bag perched on the hall table. When I peeked inside, a flood of tears blurred my eyes. I struggled to finally get the words out.

"Oh my god, these are the black jade earrings I had swooned over. But, Malisa had said she could never part with them because they carried such sentimental value for her."

My hubby offered me the tissue box and a warm hug.

* *The North-West Frontier Province (NWFP) was a province of British India and later of Pakistan. It was established on November 9, 1901. Short form 'Frontier' was used for convenience.*

ZOHRA ZOBERI

Zohra Zoberi's short stories, poetry and plays are published in numerous anthologies in Canada and the U.S. Two books to her credit are *True Colours* (poetry) and *Window Shopping...For Lasting Love*. Zohra has produced stage productions addressing social issues: cyber bullying, sexual harassment, women's abuse and marital concerns. Work in progress is her memoir titled *The Other I.*

RENA FLANNIGAN

Researching for a Trip on the Rhine

I love reading maps and imagining where I'll go next. This is quite amusing for me because although I did not care for geography at school, now I love the adventure of new places. I always loved history—I sometimes wonder if that was an escape from reality though, living in the past and not facing the future?

When I say I enjoyed history I don't mean all the dates we had to remember and quote in school. They are important but only if history is to be your future career. I have had the good fortune to visit many places, and when I see advertisements for holidays here and there, my memory takes me back over the miles (or kilometres) I covered working as a tour manager and guide. So many other destinations remain in my mind to dream of, knowing they will never materialize. I am so thankful for memories of them all now that I am retired, and memories are all I have.

Some people have amazing imaginations about murder and mayhem, about angels and romance, so many different things. I am not that imaginative until I get a map in my possession and then I am gone with the fairies! One time I was booked to be a tour guide in Germany sailing down the Rhine River, which meant doing research so that I would be able to talk with clients as if I knew what I was talking about—not much chance! Mostly a lot of trial and error at times, but fun with the right people. We would often explore together in the end.

According to a German legend, Lorelei, a beautiful maiden, was sitting way up on the high cliffs, at the bend of the Rhine. In despair over a faithless lover, she threw herself into the river and later transformed into a Siren who would lure sailors to their deaths. With the upcoming tour I imagined already seeing and hearing the mythical Siren at the bend of the river. I wondered if some of the sailors had been imbibing as they sailed past the Siren. Naturally, while I was going down the Rhine Valley I would taste some of the many wines the area is famous for.

I pictured King Ludwig's Castle, so reminiscent of the Palace of Versailles in France. All the gold and glitter, the marvellous fountains and the incredible flower beds in the vast gardens. Too bad for him he went mad. Now people from all over the world can see the masterpiece he created and that I was not destined to see. Neither it nor Versailles! My tour was cancelled about two weeks before we were to sail on that trip. So disappointing.

I wondered at the placement of many of the castles as well, and my practical mind would start to work overtime. Contemplating: *How did the builders get the supplies up there, what did they do for plumbing? What if the housekeeper forgot the milk, did she have to run into town to get some? Did they make their own candles? Were the Royal bums cold as they hung over the open toilet pits?* Can you imagine seeing some Lord of the Manor with his derriere dangling there? So many things to consider, maybe they used "porcelain gosunders?" Luckily I didn't lose too much sleep over the questions.

Seeing the locations of some of the magnificent castles perched in the most impossible places leads me to think again, *when it is very windy, do the walls shake?* The peasants who did the dirty work of maintenance were not "hewers of logs" so wood would have to be brought up to the castle. Did they use pack animals? I am worn out just thinking about it all and have decided instead of worrying about their hard labours and transport, I will transport myself, not in imagination but in reality, to the kitchen and make a cup of tea!

RENA FLANNIGAN

From Top to Bottom in a Spiral

No one ever thinks they will be doubling back on themselves when they enter a tunnel, yet this is exactly what they would do if they travelled by train in the beautiful Western Canadian Mountains. Nor would they be aware that a man took his life as a result of the construction of this incredible tunnel.

When visiting that area, it is easy to visualize Jeanette MacDonald being serenaded by Nelson Eddy when he sang "When I'm Calling You" or *"Rose Marie,"* featured in the film of the same name, *Rose Marie*. One can almost hear the songs echoing through the vast beauty of the mountains. In this film, these mountains look rather phoney, but what a thrill it was to watch the movie in its day. The scenery is so outstanding and is exactly what most people imagine when they think of Canada. The tour posters are deceptive though; they give the impression that Canada is full of snow-capped peaks. Something I found out later was that the mountains in the movie were more likely to be in the States, and not in Canada.

There are seven ranges of mountains, not only the Rockies, to be crossed. These ranges are so intricate that trestle bridges were erected to link one mountain to another, until it came to the Yoho Valley, where only a tunnel could service traffic across the area.

Rarely does one see much publicity promoting the prairies: Manitoba, Saskatchewan or Alberta. Yet these provinces are more important than the mountains. They are the "bread-basket" of

Canada and, of course, where would one find a better piece of beef if they did not buy it from Alberta? We also use and export grain from the prairies. However, so far no one has attempted to eat the granite of the Rockies. That would be hard on the teeth if nothing else.

The eastern side of the foothills where the mountains begin is quite deceptive, because they do start there. However, the ranges can be seen from Calgary, only eighty miles away, I visited Alberta in 1954 for the first time. It was so exhilarating for me to physically see this area. I have been fortunate to travel through the Rockies several times since, and each visit was just as exciting. My childhood fantasy was coming true in a sense, being among these powerful behemoths and "hearing" Nelson Eddy serenading me, in my imagination. Why not me?

After crossing the Rockies, the Great Divide and many other ranges, the Canadian Pacific Railway (CPR) realized there was no way to traverse the Yoho Valley without the convenience of a tunnel. How was this to be achieved? So, an engineer from Switzerland was hired. Who better than the Swiss to build tunnels? The engineer knew the only way through the rock was to circle down, literally, inside the high mountain, so he designed the Spiral Tunnel. What an engineering feat this is, incredible both for travel and also as a spectator to watch a train as it enters the tunnel at the top of the peak, disappears, and eventually emerges at the bottom. As one turns around to see the train disappear again underground, there it is once more, continuing to the other side of the road!

Car passengers, hikers and train travellers all gaze in wonder at the scene. There is not only a tunnel through the mountain, but also one under the road. It is fascinating, and a marvellous piece of engineering.

The construction of this tunnel was started from a high point and from the lower reaches at the same time, in the 1800s. Many lives were lost during the construction, mostly Chinese workers who had been specifically brought to Canada and the United States to build railways and tunnels where needed. If one worker was killed during excavation, the company just brought in another "body." This is a sad reflection on the history of both countries, but eventually the tunnel neared completion. During an inspection, the engineer checked the progress. Imagine his shock when he estimated that neither section was aligned, as the joining approached top with bottom.

We often hear the old adage, "read the small print." Sadly this brilliant man did not—somehow he misread the plans. He thought his magnificent creation was way out of kilter and committed suicide as a result. He misinterpreted the distance between the two ends of the track and thought it could not be corrected. In fact, the tunnel was not as far out of alignment as he surmised. It turned out to be only about a metre (three feet); however, he read a much larger difference between the two ends. At this stage it was still possible to correct the alignment. It was a sad ending for someone who created such a masterpiece. He never lived to receive accolades for his amazing accomplishment.

It would be interesting to know how many people who have travelled through the tunnel over the years have even the slightest clue as to the cost of lives: of the workers and the engineer himself.

In the "hereafter," does he look down at the many tourists who think his creation is truly an incredible piece of engineering? All the while they survey, in wonder, as they see both ends of the train while it is traversing the mountain. The tunnel could rate as one of the world's wonders. In the mid-1800s, the first train departed from Toronto in the east, to Vancouver in the west. The official joining of the tracks was marked by a "Last Spike" at Craigalachie. It would indeed be nice to believe the engineer looks down with pride seeing his masterpiece.

To give CPR its due, one hundred years later they erected a monument on railway lands honouring the Chinese workers. This is located at the sports palace known originally as the SkyDome in Toronto, later renamed the Rogers Centre. The monument is inscribed in English, French and Chinese and has pieces of the great Rockies standing very proudly beside the miniature trestle bridge. This represents the incredible trestles built to cross from mountain to mountain. The original bridges were a work of art. Built in the 1800s, they are still serving the railway nearly two hundred years later.

RENA FLANNIGAN

Rena Flannigan chose to be a Canadian as a youngster and has lived in Ontario since 1952. Her careers have included tailoress, fur finisher, vice-principal of a private school, self-employed business owner, tour manager and guide, champion speedskater/tennis-player/skier/ballroom- and Latin dancing trophy winner. Now an author.

BALA MENON

It's All in the Mind, or Is It?

Hush, little baby, don't say a word,
I will have to kill you with my sword
Up goes the spider, up on the spout
Up goes this blade, into your snout.

The child screamed as the six-inch blade went into her nose, slicing the delicate nostrils apart, blood spraying like a thin fountain, into the sinus and up into the brain. She shook as if she was being electrocuted and then fell silent. Dead.

*****

Now, dear reader, you must be wondering what is happening here? I must explain, I will explain. First, let me tell you that Sarah is not a baby; she is a monster-child of about four years old.

Our story began some sixty years ago, in the northern Ontario village of Gravenhurst, in the beautiful Muskoka Lake region. There was a wonderful little house, painted blue, just off Steamship Bay Road, with aluminum siding and windows. It had a small porch that looked onto one of the pretty little lakes in the area called Sterling Lake, which teemed with fish and was surrounded by ancient woods.

A little distance away was the Barkway Pioneer cemetery that, I understand, is now closed. There were big trees there and I was buried near one of those huge elms.

"She killed me," I told my wife, pointing at baby Sarah. "Everybody in the Gravenhurst of the 1960s knew that she killed me, robbed me and fled the province."

"What are you saying, George? Do you have any idea what you are saying? Sarah is our grand-daughter," my wife remonstrated.

"Her name was Tamara and she was my neighbour," I insisted. "She feigned interest in me, coming into the house alone at odd hours when her parents were off at work or leaping over the short, trimmed boundary hedge whenever she felt like it—with us ending up on the couch and kissing and cuddling and I thought we had a good thing going. I was even thinking of proposing to her, once my job as a boat machinist at the Penetanguishene docks was made permanent and I could stop some of my quick-money deals.

"However, one evening, one dreary winter evening, I told her I didn't like the things I was hearing about her at the marina and why some of the ruffians there were talking about her as an easy girl. 'They use the choicest words to describe you, Tamara,' I told her. 'I don't want anything to do with you anymore!' She did not utter a word. Minutes later, she crept behind me, hitting me on the head several times with a claw hammer and I bled to death in front of the fireplace."

I reached up to feel the bump on the back of my head, a bump my parents said I had when I was born in Pembroke in 1963, nine months after my murder.

"It's all coming back to me, Lisa, in bits and pieces, all those little fragments of dreams from many years, now getting stronger: a kaleidoscope coalescing into solid memories."

"You are beginning to have those nightmares during the day, George," Lisa frowned and shook her head. "Where are you getting all these fancy words? Let me call the doctor. You must see him again and ask for a new prescription. You are going on and on like some Tibetan or Bhutanese lama about a past life. Or some Hindu born-again excuse. What nonsense!"

"I am not becoming unhinged, Lisa. I even remember the dress she was wearing fifty-nine years ago. It is all coming into sharper focus. It was a red skirt with a black and white check blouse. It was hazy for a long time, but in recent days … in recent days …" I was becoming a little agitated by now.

"George, don't forget we are living with our son and his family," my wife grumbled. "You know we are broke and have no other place to stay. You sold our home, destroyed our savings with your rotten investments and now this … this ranting about our only grand-daughter."

I rummaged through my drawers and took out the *Gravenhurst Post* edition, dated January 26, 1963, which I stole from the Gravenhurst Public Library some years ago. Although wrapped in plastic, the paper was yellowing and becoming brittle. I opened it carefully to page 3 and showed the brief report to Lisa. "Read. See what I told you."

Drug Dealing Local Mechanic Killed

Mechanic John M. Glover, 26, a part-time employee at the Penetanguishene docks, was bludgeoned to death with a claw hammer in the living room of his home on the bank of Sterling Lake last evening. Sheriff Moe Girard said preliminary evidence pointed out that it was a woman behind the killing and that robbery was the motive.

Glover had no bank accounts and is believed to have hoarded a considerable sum of cash in his bedroom. Floorboards were found removed and a part of the wall had been torn down. Some $100 notes were found behind the wall. Glover was known to the police and was apparently dealing in bulk quantities of marijuana and involved with out-of-town gangs. However, he was said to be trying to turn his life around. All rooms had been ransacked. Investigations are continuing. Glover has no surviving next of kin.

Glover will be buried in the public corner of the municipal cemetery, far away from the private or reserved burial grounds.

"Look, that's my picture in the report. See the forehead, and just look at the nose. They are just like mine."

"Come on, George." Lisa was exasperated. "When you were 26, it was 1989 and we got married that year. I don't know where you are getting these ideas from. I must call the doctor now. And...and what, you were a drug peddler?"

"Yes, I was 26 when I was first killed in 1963. Yes, I was 26 when we got married in 1989. There is no connection between the two," I tried to explain. "Today's me was born on January 25, 1963—the day John Glover was killed. Don't you see any link? Why is your mind so closed?"

Lisa doesn't understand. What I feel today is a shared, unconscious bond with myself in a past life. Life and death are cyclical, like our seasons. We come and go and come again. Since childhood, I have had this acute pain on the back of my head, whenever I felt somebody coming up behind me. In recent days, when sitting on the porch or puttering about in the garden I suddenly feel the saltiness of blood gurgling in my throat, its sting in my eyes, the choking on my vomit as I see myself lying on some shabby carpet a long time ago. These feelings are real for me. I cannot grasp them, they are like flashes of light and shadow, with angst and panic rising and ebbing.

I also cannot explain how I have become so eloquent in my speech, when I have been known throughout my life to be a taciturn character with a limited vocabulary. However, I know for sure that John Glover was a loquacious man who could hold the interest of his listeners. On my occasional evening visits now to the pub in our Orangeville neighbourhood, I can hold forth a stimulating conversation on any subject and quash all arguments uttering words which few people understand. It is no wonder that Lisa seems so worried. She keeps asking: "Why here, why now, why you?"

This is the same question I ask myself: "Why here, why now, why me?" It is an ontological problem for which there is no interpretation.

Gravenhurst Post, edition dated June 5, 1963:

Trail Cold In Local Mechanic's Murder

Sheriff Moe Girard told reporters yesterday that the trail had gone cold in the murder of Sterling Lake resident John Glover, who was killed in his home on January 26 this year. His neighbour, 30-year-old Tamara McGregor, who disappeared on the day of the murder, is the prime suspect and is believed to have fled the province with a large amount of cash, taken from Glover, a local mechanic with gangland connections.

Her parents have no information and haven't heard from her for months. In fact, they said they were happy that she had gone away from their lives. 'Yes, our daughter was wild, uncontrollable,' Monty McGregor, who works for the City Parks Department, said. 'She was into drugs, into men and we don't know what else. We have nothing to do with her.'

Gerard said he has had no new information about her whereabouts from police forces across the country.

All these years on, it's as if John Glover had never existed. I have checked. In Gravenhurst, the little blue house is long gone. In the sixties, many houses and surrounding areas were taken over for a resort and an upscale residential community. Today's Gravenhurst is not the sleepy town it was at that time.

I feel deeply within me that Tamara died four years ago, somewhere in the Maritimes and she has reincarnated as my granddaughter. I have no doubt about it. See the way Sarah angles her face when she looks at me. She doesn't blink. She stares into me and through me and I have to take deep breaths to ward off panic attacks. I believe she is the same evil soul born in the flesh again, a spirit that has just donned a new body, like a garment. Strong emotions can travel with the soul through many births and be part of the transmigration process. I tell you, Sarah's soul is fixated on that murderous moment of decades ago, and now waiting for a spark.

By the age of two or so, she had learnt to spit at me whenever I got close to her and to poke me in the eye when I lifted her from her crib. She is cunning, yes. She snarls at me like a vicious wolf when nobody is looking; oh, the sweet little thing, the darling little girl with the pretty brown curls, the angelic Sarah.

You don't have to worry, however, dear reader. There is no need to call the police or shrinks or asylum wardens or whatever. I have not killed Sarah, although I fantasize about it often. She is now prancing around in the other room, playing with her devilish rattles and noise-making toys and only God knows what is coursing through her brain. However, I will never touch her, never coo into her ears, never play grandfather games with her.

I know that one day she will kill me. Again.

*****

The bell rang. It was our son Thomas and his wife Janet returning from one of their many recent, extended outings. They have been wandering a bit too much these days, leaving us to baby sit their daughter.

"Hey Dad, hey Mom," Thomas called out. He sounded exuberant. "I've got the Marine Engineer's job I applied for a month ago. And guess what? We have to move away from Orangeville. We've found a wonderful new home. You'll both love it. It is big and bright and Sarah will have a lot of space to run around as she gets older. We just signed off on all the documents today."

"Oh," I said, "Oh," while my wife clucked around in the kitchen, putting on the kettle and taking the cups out along with some ginger snaps for tea as Janet went to check on Sarah.

"This home is just off Steamship Bay Road," Thomas was exultant as he circled around the room, keen to hear words of approval. "And it is right on the shore of the beautiful little Sterling Lake. It's really pretty with stunning views of the awesome countryside in Gravenhurst, you know in the Muskoka region."

BALA MENON

Journalist-artist-historian-storyteller: Bala has worked for newspapers in India/Middle East and is Editor-in-Chief of the Voice Media Group in Toronto. He co-authored *Spice & Kosher: Exotic Cuisine of the Cochin Jews* and *The Jewish Gandhi of Cochin: A Biography of A.B. Salem*. He also co-edited *Rhapsody Lane: A Collection by Flower City Writers*. He is a member of the Canadian Journalists' Association, Courtney Park Writers' Group, Brampton Writers' Guild and others.

SHEILA E. TUCKER

The March

After that afternoon, I refused to play hide and seek ever again.

It was thirty years ago. I was eight and my twin cousins were nine, and we used to hang out at Grandpa's house after school until our parents came to collect us. Jimmy and Al were always physical, which was good for a couch potato like me. As an only child, at home I used to read a lot or play solitaire on the fireside rug with my dad's cards. My cousins, on the other hand, bounced, sprinted, wrestled, and climbed everything in sight. With them, I clambered up trees, rollerbladed and biked, and learned how to do the doggy paddle.

On this one sunny afternoon, we decided to play hide and seek. I closed my eyes and counted to fifty, then went looking for them. We were down by the old quarry: a junkyard paradise for kids our age. Some of the treasures included rusted trams and sacks piled high with dust and dirt. Even old scales could be found. When we were younger still, I'd play shopkeeper and weigh mud pies that my customer-cousins would buy with pebbles and lop at the crumbling brick tower.

"...Forty-nine, fifty!"

I searched in the usual places. Abandoned old vehicles, roofless huts and through the sand dunes. No sign of either of them. I ventured further afield, across the disintegrating rail tracks and around wild shrubs and bushes.

"Al? Jimmy?"

Only a blackbird answered my call.

Returning to the dunes, I wandered across them and down the slope to the quarry. Panting, I stepped over an ancient, half-fallen fence and headed toward an opening I'd never seen before, jumping when a series of thumps made me swirl around. The fence was collapsing like dominos, causing the dry earth to spew clouds of dust.

I turned back and entered what I realized was a tunnel, and quickly walked to a curve at the far end. Peering around the corner, I saw the blackest black of darkness I'd ever seen. Who knew how far that went? A click startled me into looking back at the opening and the daylight beyond.

"Al?"

Silence.

"Jimmy?"

Nothing.

Returning my glance to the darkness, I suddenly realized I was mistaken. It wasn't so black along there after all. A dim red light was glowing from beyond the following bend, so I made my way towards it, trying and failing to see where I was walking. However, nothing tripped me up; it was gravelly, but flat.

The air was clammy and cold. And I'd never experienced silence like that. I suddenly hoped I wouldn't bump into Gollum or get lost in Middle-earth. I began to wish I wasn't there.

I reached the next corner. The red light was stronger now, and as I felt my way along a curve and turned another bend I realized I was in a large, stone hall, at the opening of one of five entrances. The other four tunnels looked just like the one I came out of. They were all leading into darkness from the glow in this pentagon-shaped space. I looked up to see where the light was coming from, but in fact there was no lamp, no torch or candle. The dull-red light seemed to shine by itself, all around me.

I placed a hand on the damp wall of my corridor, not wanting to get it confused with the others. Even now, thirty years later, I thank myself for having the sense to do this. But as I did so, I heard a clomping, as of many people in many pairs of boots, which in fact is exactly what appeared next. I gasped as a long line of men in baggy old clothes, and with skeletal faces, marched out of one dark tunnel and into an opposite one.

None of them turned to look at me. With their eyes staring straight ahead, and with seemingly immobile heads and shoulders, they trooped out of one tunnel, legs moving in unison, and wordlessly marched into another. The line seemed endless, and when they had finally gone, I realized I was petrified with fear and almost literally frozen as well. That's when I looked into the corridor they'd exited. There was one last man, standing motionless and silent halfway along this tunnel, his eyes boring into me, without seeming to really see me. I remember those eyes like yesterday: unblinking, with some sort of yellow glow about them, almost is if they were lit with neon from the inside. His thin mouth was a straight slit across his face.

I inched backward, slowly and as quietly as possible, shaking with fear and cold. After what seemed like an eternity, I reached the corner and then the previous corner, at which point I turned and ran like a hunted rabbit towards the round opening, towards the upper earth I knew, towards the sunlight that was now streaming into the manmade crevice.

Speeding over the collapsed fence, up and up to the quarry's top, and even then not stopping until I reached Grandpa's.

To my fury, there were my cousins, lying on the rug playing dominoes.

"Where were you? That wasn't funny!"

Alarmed, they gaped at me. I could feel myself shaking violently. Grandpa held my shoulders and kneeled down. "What's wrong?" he asked.

But I couldn't tell them. All I could do was cry.

SHEILA E. TUCKER

Not Today

Just look at her—perched on the old log in the village park, deep in thought at seven years old.

Her mom is on a nearby bench, knitting and occasionally looking up to check on her daughter's whereabouts, but she needn't worry. The child is going nowhere. Not today.

We all know her dad was posted to Syria. He left yesterday afternoon. Many of us stood along the street to wave him off. He kissed Maureen and hugged little Karen tightly before getting into his friend's car for a ride into the city.

We understand, of course, that military folks sign up with this in mind, that they may be sent to a war zone. And even though it's a peacekeeping mission, we know what can happen.

It's up to us in the village now, to keep an eye on Garth's family. We'll take turns to visit once in while, not too many of us all at once, but to reassure them of our love and respect. We'll offer to babysit when Maureen needs to go somewhere, and we'll invite Karen to sleep over with our children some weekends. Even though it may be only a street away, kids love sleepovers.

I wonder what is going on in that lovely girl's mind. Sometimes, we underestimate youngsters and forget that when we're watching the news, they're taking it all in too: the bombs, guns, bodies under sheets. Children often stop asking questions after a while. But they know about the cruelty of the world, the danger, the grief of starving parents of skeletal babies and the pain of boys with blown-off legs. Ironic that movies are rated. We forget that worse is on the screen in our living rooms.

Karen is staring off into space. Is she scared? Deep-down angry? Quietly revisiting those television scenes of the Middle East?

For a normally boisterous kid, she's very different this morning. I see Maureen now gazing at her thoughtfully. She's putting her knitting away. I see her call something to Karen, with no response. She calls again, and Karen shakes her head and stays where she is. She doesn't appear to want to get up.

Not today.

SHEILA E. TUCKER

Sheila E. Tucker worked as an editor/graphic designer for an international firm. Her work is published in anthologies, newspapers and e-zines, and a memoir, *Rag Dolls and Rage*, was launched late 2019. Sheila recently wrote and illustrated a children's book, *On A Higher Hill,* the first in a series under pen name S.E. Tee.

facebook.com/groups/setee & ragdollsandrage.com &
shieldyourself.net /

DAVID L. TUCKER

Picture This!
(Excerpt from upcoming novel)

Chapter 2
2017

My thin sandals felt like hot coals as I stepped out of the cab onto the scorching sidewalk. I'd arrived in Mayfair in the middle of a prolonged heat wave, my body dry kindling as I humped my backpack and suit bag from the taxi. Still, after airport security and an economy flight, I was just glad the ordeal was over.

I squinted at my hotel's red brick façade; its Victorian railings decked out in international flags and colourful pots of flowers. Generations of kings and cabbages had stayed in this luxurious ecosphere, so it seemed fitting that a silver-haired doorman with the Biblical name Gabriel embroidered on his uniform should usher me through its Pearly Gates.

"G' day, sir," he said, cheerily.

I nodded, uncomfortably. I wasn't used to having doors opened for me. I always figured a practical joke waited on the other side. Like Gabriel was actually Cerberus in disguise, presiding over the Gates of Hell...

I'd read stories about Brexit Britain, heard about the hard times, seen pictures of shuttered libraries, police stations and community pools, been aware of public parks sold off to developers. But here, in Mayfair, steps from the posh Savile Club, there were no hints of hardship. This was a glittering, gold-plated mirage in the middle of a Banksy's Dismaland.*

The hotel lobby offered welcome respite from the sweltering heat. I crossed its cool expanse of white marble to the paneled mahogany check-in counter. Dressed in old jeans and a wrinkled tee, surrounded by well-heeled business types, I felt like a refugee visiting a country club. I was surprised when the manager, a short, stocky man, named Burrows, manners as polished as his black Oxfords, addressed me by name.

"Process of elimination, Mr. Fredrick," he explained, motioning to my backpack displaying the Air Canada tag. "Canadian flights arrive in the morning. It's nearly 11:00 and we have only one Canadian guest checking in today." Burrows would have made a good Hercules Poirot. All he lacked was a waxed moustache.

"Afternoon tea is served from 2:00 'till 4:30," Burrows informed, as I signed in. "I've reserved you and your guest one of our very best tables."

I thanked him then followed a tall, skinny bellhop, as he trolleyed my few worldly possessions across to a bank of gleaming brass lifts. One floor up, we proceeded down a wainscoted corridor lined with antiques and expensive oils, my sandals sinking mutely into the deep pile. The young man described the hotel's storied history, but I wasn't absorbing much. My mind was on Anne. That afternoon, I was seeing my little cousin for the first time in thirty years.

I was anxious about our reunion. After all these years, I was still clinging to a childhood crush. Simone Beauvoir might have called it existential vulnerability: putting faith in another to make one's own life meaningful. Or maybe it was just simple insanity. Whatever you want to call it, I was on a mission, determined to see it through.

So much time had passed since our days at Clearview, my uncle's farm in Caledon. A lot of cubic feet had flowed under the proverbial bridge. Was she still a Pre-Raphaelite portrait come to life, all flaming red hair and emerald eyes? Based on her Instagram posts, she'd aged well, not that I ever put stock in curated media.

The reality was that we were now both over forty. Could afternoon tea and cucumber sandwiches reclaim lost youth? Nabokov once said you're always home in your past. For me, the past was a permanent address.

As the bellhop opened my door, I noticed a security guard standing outside number two twelve, directly across the hall. Scary-looking dude. Stuffed into a suit a size too small, with a face torn from Hieronymus Bosch's Hellscape. Most likely here protecting some doped-up diva or Russian oligarch. I hoped whoever it was, they were worth dying for.

My room channeled the hotel's jazz age heritage, an Art Deco mash-up of rosewood, geometric fabrics and striped prints. The room was off a small vestibule adjoining a green marble bathroom with polished, chrome fixtures. Beside the canopy bed, a complimentary bottle of champagne chilled in a silver bucket. I pictured sharing it with Anne.

Wishful thinking…

I tipped the bellhop and locked the door after him. Through the peephole, I could see Hieronymus staring at my door. The guy gave me the creeps. I secured the chain, just in case he became any more interested.

I was tired and thirsty. My flight had been delayed, followed by six hours of cramped knees, screaming kids, bad food and stale air. I switched on the bathroom light, desperate for a glass of water. In the large circular mirror stood a stranger, his tired face etched with fault lines and silver stubble. I'd morphed into a cabbage patch doll, the top of my head a tangle of greying, brown hair. Where was the boyish charm? The sparkle in the eye…? That semblance of self-confidence…? Mine was an unfinished face, roughly sketched around the eyes and mouth. Some might even call it a blank canvas, the kind that parents paint their own frustrated dreams on.

What was I thinking, coming here, blowing meagre savings on this marble mausoleum?! All for a childhood-crush-turned-midlife-crisis…

I turned out the light, feeling like a tire with a slow leak: deflated. I flopped onto the Egyptian cotton thread count, desperate for some shuteye. But I tossed and turned, fearing I'd oversleep. Anne would be arriving soon.

I should have arranged to meet tomorrow…!

Just blocks away, Anne ran a gallery, the proverbial uptown girl. And here's me, the country cousin, scraping by on government arts grants. Apart from our twelve-percent shared DNA and a few childhood memories, what could we possibly have in common?

Did I *really* believe Anne would drop everything and move in with me? Or that I'd get to exhibit my work here in the art capital of Europe?! Would a few days visit change anything…? I should I have listened to my buddy, Rob. He said going to London would be like acting out a Russian novel, the kind that ends badly.

I told myself Rob was just jealous, resentful my pretty cousin had never paid him the slightest attention. In fact, I'd told him to get stuffed. Said I'd spent my life playing it safe. Avoiding pain to the point of numbness. For once, I was going to take a chance.

But now, I was scared shitless. I really had stepped outside my comfort zone.

I peeled myself off the bed, intending to do some push-ups and planks, or maybe go for a jog around the block. I needed to get my energy back, boost my self-confidence. Instead, I settled for a cool bath. As I stretched out in the long, porcelain tub, immersing in Dead Sea salt, my mind was a jumble of thoughts.

As kids, Anne and I had bonded over art books in her father's wood-paneled study. There, we soaked up new worlds and subversive ideas. Art was our journey into the deep woods in search of magic. It offered fantasy, an escape, a new way of seeing.

With my cousin's encouragement, I took up sketching. At first, my drawings were an embarrassment but, gradually, they improved. I even found I had a talent for portraiture after Anne modeled for me. I think she thrived on the attention, given her parents gave her so little. I enjoyed drawing her, capturing the symmetry of that perfect oval face and the bright, sparkling eyes. Her many moods. She consumed my sketchbook. And my thoughts.

Thirty years…! So much has changed…

Clearview is gone, bulldozed into a shopping mall. My parents are old and frail. Aunt Ethyl is deceased, victim of a heart attack. Uncle Glen, former real estate agent turned property magnate, now resides here, in London. So does his daughter, Anne, a graduate of the prestigious Courtauld Institute of the Arts and current owner of that posh Mayfair gallery. Oh, did I mention she's married—but recently separated—from a London solicitor…?

Me…? Older but no wiser. Still trapped in my past. I studied fine art at a local community college. Acquired an appreciation for the finer things in life. The kind of beauty you could only get to admire from afar.

After Anne's family moved to London, I wrote, but she never replied. I never understood why she'd ghost me. Sure, we had that falling out. But it was nothing serious—not enough to sever ties, in any case. Did her folks find my one naughty sketch of her and forbid her writing? Or did she simply decide to move on? Anne had been the one person I could confide in. And I felt abandoned.

I went on to study art at a local college. Acquired an appreciation for the finer things in life, the art you'll never afford.

My first show garnered two sales, both to friends motivated out of pity. I was forced to borrow money from my parents, and I saw that resigned *I told you so* look in their eyes.

Then the digital revolution arrived. I tried my hand at photography, explored digital media, even experimented with sculpture. Nothing clicked. In the end, I returned to painting. I liked that it was part of a tradition extending from the earliest cave paintings to the latest works by Doig, Dumas and Richter. For me, the medium captured everything, the base *and* the sublime.

To pay the rent, I painted reproductions, familiar works by

Monet, Renoir and Van Gogh, then sold them on consignment through poster shops or else on e-Bay. I got by but the joy of creating ebbed. I questioned my talent, saw my life framed in failure. I retreated to my studio apartment, avoiding family and friends, unwilling to face their judgment.

Then, out of the blue, Anne connected with me online. I'd never expected to hear from her again. We texted first, then spoke over the phone. There was no mistaking that voice, sweet and tart, like lemon squeezed over dark chocolate. She was newly separated. Apparently, her hubby, Wayne, had charmed a paralegal out of her legal briefs. Then he'd abruptly disappeared with her, along with most of the money, leaving Anne saddled in debt.

She spoke of regrets. Waxed poetic about happier times. Said I'd been her anchor. That we'd been cut adrift, separated by a metaphorical ocean. She described herself as "a rudderless ship in search of safe harbour." Said she wanted to make up for lost time, if I was still willing.

I booked a flight to Heathrow that same afternoon.

The day we agreed to meet, a Peter Doig retrospective was opening at the Tate Modern. I managed the last pair of available tickets. They cost me a small fortune, but I didn't care. It was something Anne and I could share, like old times in her father's study, a reminder of how art had brought us together. I printed off the vouchers and stuffed them into my new suit, the one I'd bought at Harry's during one of his annual half-price sales.

I checked my watch, resting by the side of the tub.

2:15! She'll be here already!

I clambered out of the bath and reached for my suit. That's when I realized I'd forgotten to pack dress shoes. Anne would notice. I slipped on my scuffed loafers, the ones I'd planned to jettison in the garbage at the end of the week.

In my rush out the door, I collided with a maid coming out of room two twelve. She was pushing a laundry hamper piled high with linen and towels. I stammered an apology, but before I could finish, I heard the phone ringing in my room. Sure enough, it was Anne.

"I'm downstairs waiting," she said, sounding impatient. As I closed the door again, I noticed the maid had completely vanished. And, so had Hieronymus.

* Banksy is a famous UK-based street artist and political activist whose real name and identity remain unconfirmed and the subject of speculation. His Dismaland was a dystopian theme park.

DAVID L. TUCKER

David L. Tucker is an award-winning television producer/director and writer whose shows for CBC's *The Nature of Things* have garnered multiple international television awards including a Gemini. His short-story collection, *One Way Ticket,* won an Oakville Arts Council literary award. *Picture This!* is his upcoming novel. He is also a professor emeritus at Toronto's Ryerson University.

KONRAD BRINCK

The Berlin Airlift: 1947-1949

Berlin survived many crises in the twentieth century. After the Second World War it was the front line of defence to tyranny and expansion of Soviet Communism. The most historic crisis was the blockade of Berlin. Following the oppressive years of the Third Reich, and the bombing of the city by the allied forces, it now faced a blockade that threatened to starve its citizens into oblivion.

Imagine, feeding a city of 2.8 million hungry people without the ability to bring any food into the city by car, train or boat. As a result, the only option left was flying it in, making the task infinitely harder.

This exact scenario is what the United States, Great Britain, and France faced in 1946, with the city of Berlin.

The Berlin Airlift was a period in history, in which all three allies were forced by the Soviet Union to feed Berlin's population, by flying in all food and supplies to help Berliners survive. It is considered one of the most remarkable aviation feats of all time, considering that a fully loaded plane had to touch down every three minutes, just to keep pace with the food needs of the city.

At the height of the operation an allied aircraft landed in Berlin every minute. The major Berlin airfields were Tempelhof, Gatow, and Tegel, which was built by army engineers and Berlin volunteers in forty-nine days, inside the French sector. The runway was the longest in Europe, enabling heavy bombers to land, if the blockade should continue. Float-planes landed on the Havel River which became the fourth "airport" of Berlin.

Life For The Berliners

Survival was extremely hard. In the beginning, there was about a month's worth of supplies, however, stockpiles were dwindling. The airlift had not reached its predicted consumption rate as yet, and starvation was near. In the winter there was little fuel to run industry, let alone heat the homes of Berliners. Residents soon found themselves learning what grasses and other plants could be eaten for food. People rummaged through garbage cans, but soon found that there wasn't enough to go around. Circumstances were dire, but still they realized that their suffering would be better than succumbing to Soviet control. They remembered the previous treatment given them by Soviet soldiers. They had stolen valuables, systematically stripping industry of all of the necessary equipment and shipping it to Moscow. German women were being raped. German scientists and engineers were sent to Moscow and forced to reveal German technological secrets.

Starvation was a better choice than Soviet treatment. When it was decided that an airlift would be attempted, Berlin's Lord Mayor Ernst Reuter held a public rally in support of the effort. Germans would suffer and sacrifice to make it work. The German resolve was strong, even during a desperate situation.

The Soviets extended a "benevolent" hand to the citizens of West Berlin. They offered them the option of using their West Berlin food ration cards, in East Berlin. As ration cards could only be used once, this would have amounted to a choice between Soviet and Western rations.

The USSR intended this to become a "vote by ration" card which, of course, should establish them as the reliable patron of all Berliners. However, the citizens of West Berlin did not turn against the Western allies—instead, they resented the USSR for placing them into the blockade in the first place. Only twenty thousand Berliners, less than seven percent of Berlin's population, accepted their offer. It was seen as a humiliating defeat by the Soviets as the motto "Rather dead than red" grew as a battle cry among the starving population of Berlin.

My Family During The Berlin Airlift: Hamstering

I don't recall the Airlift but I vividly remember all the stories that were told. Accounts of suffering, the ingenuity required to stay alive under such difficult circumstances and of a community pulling together and supporting each other. It was neighbour helping neighbour, in order to ensure everybody would survive this trying time, after suffering through the bitter end of the war and with the bombardment of the city. The residents had to endure barbaric treatment by the Russian soldiers and the torturous wait for husbands and sons to return, not knowing if they had been killed or were held as prisoners of war (POWs).

My father returned home after a short time as a POW and was happy to find work. When I was born after the war, things were starting to look up with signs of normal life returning to our family and the citizens of Berlin.

Then, in June of 1947, the Soviets announced that they would temporarily close all roads, waterways and railway tracks to and from Berlin for "repairs and upgrades" of the infrastructure in the Soviet Zone. Everybody knew what that meant. They were trying to annex the city and force the Allies to retreat. During the first months of the blockade, life seemed to continue normally even though rations were cut significantly. Life was more difficult but still liveable. When supplies ran out, my father lost his job and food became almost impossible to obtain.

That's when a new activity was born and it was called "hamstering." The roads to East Berlin were still open, the subway still crossed into the East and people were free to travel into the Soviet-occupied zone where farmers were still producing food for their population. Hamstering meant traveling to the East and bartering valuables for food. Anything and everything was bartered, from the family jewels to offering to work on a farm for food. Sometimes my father would stay away for a whole week. He would walk from village to village, sleep in haystacks or work on a farm for a few days. He was not alone: thousands of men went to the East to hamster.

This was not without danger since the transporting of goods was strictly prohibited. If caught by the Soviet or East-German guards you were thrown into jail and everything would be confiscated. The guards were not eager to catch people coming into the Soviet Zone, since the importation of items like jewellery, silverware, porcelain, carpets and other goods was legal. Exporting food items was illegal since food was rationed in the East and not permitted to be brought into Berlin. It was considered smuggling and was a punishable offence.

Anyone with a suitcase or backpack was ordered to open it and if "illegal substances" like bread, flour, vegetables or any edible items were found, they were taken away and so was your freedom. So the most ingenious ways of smuggling food were devised. When returning home, empty suitcases were filled with firewood or worthless items while the food was hidden on your body and in your clothes.

My father told us that he was once searched by a Russian border guard while he had a sausage strapped to his groin and had dried peas in his hat. The guard didn't find them but also didn't know what to think about the useless, broken tools Dad stashed in the briefcase, as a decoy. Bread was hard to transport, so Dad went to hamster some flour. He wore a pair of regular underpants and over them a pair of long-johns. He found a farmer who gave him a sack of flour, for four days of labour and some other valuables my father offered him. To hide the flour, my father tightened the legs of the long-johns around his ankles and poured the flour into them. The farmer drove my father to the train station since it was extremely difficult to walk with fifty pounds of flour in your pants. When he got home his feet were blue from the lack of circulation.

Women did their part to keep their families fed. My mother learned gardening and how to barter for food in exchange for other goods my father had brought. Fresh milk was a most sought-after item. Ration cards only provided milk powder. My mom was constantly looking for milk to provide me with a healthy diet.

The yard in the back of our apartment complex became a vegetable garden, our balcony became a rabbit cage and even the side of the streetcar tracks were transformed into usable garden space. Every bit of available soil was used to grow food. There were no dandelions appearing in the spring. Dandelions are edible and

Berliners devoured them in salads, cooked them as vegetables or used them to fatten rabbits.

Berliners love their green spaces. There was an unwritten rule not to chop down trees, and to preserve the parks and forests, but no tree was left unpruned, no pinecone was left uncollected and the forest floor looked like it had been vacuumed.

The bombed-out buildings were a good source of firewood. Most of the old apartment buildings had wooden floors and coal was rationed, so people stripped every usable piece of wood to be used for firewood. Since gas and electricity were rationed, wood was used to heat their kitchen stoves, for cooking.

Everybody was kept busy to ensure the survival of the plucky inhabitants of this once beautiful city. It was remarkable that crime was very low, nobody plundered the little street gardens or snitched on people hamstering. The Soviet blockade brought out the best in the citizens of Berlin.

The Children Of The Airlift

Chocolate bars and candies were not high on the priority list of items the airlift provided. If residents were able to obtain an extra ration of sugar, homemade candy was there to satisfy the sweet

Pictured here are children standing next to the buildings where we lived, at the end of the runway of Tempelhof Airport. The US Air Force C-54 Skymaster was named Candy Bomber. Pic: https://www.nato.int/cps/en/natohq/declassified_136188.htm & US Air Force - public in Timeline Photos/FB.

tooth of children. Real candy or chocolate wasn't on anybody's ration sheet.

My mother loved to tell the story of the first American candy I ever ate. It was thanks to a pilot who performed a candy-drop practically next to our apartment building. This was an advantage to living next to an airport, where a plane landed every 90 seconds.

I don't believe I was the one who caught the candy, since I was too small to compete with the bigger children. It must have been Mom who stood below the approaching plane and battled older kids for the sweets that were about to fall from the sky.

The story of the "Candy Bombers," one of the most heart-warming stories of the Berlin Airlift, is that of Gail Seymour "Hal" Halvorsen. He grew up poor on farms in Utah and Idaho. He joined the United States Air Force in 1943 and was assigned to fly the Berlin Airlift.

First Airlift

Halvorsen's first 280-mile flight from Rhein-Main to Tempelhof Airport, in West Berlin, came the day after he arrived in Europe. His plane carried 138 sacks of flour for Operation Vittles. Pilots were warned to stay in the 20-mile-wide corridor and to be prepared for getting buzzed by Soviet fighters. Halvorsen's target was a city devastated by World War II bombings just a few years previously.

"As we glanced down over Berlin, it took our breath away," wrote Halvorsen. "Nothing I had read, heard or seen prepared me for the desolate, ravaged sight below ... a mottled mass of total destruction."*

On another visit, a driver took him on a jeep tour of the city. He ended up at the perimeter fence of Tempelhof, shooting pictures of planes landing. He was impressed that, though hungry, the thirty children didn't ask for anything. He had only a couple of sticks of gum, tore them in half, thinking they would fight over them. The four who took them were allowed to enjoy their treat.

When he told the kids he'd drop some candy next time, they asked in English how they'd know which plane was his? He said he would rock his wings from side to side before tossing out boxes attached to little parachutes.

With Halvorsen as good as his word, crowds of children assembled as the flights continued once a week. He soon had nicknames like *Uncle Wiggly Wings, The Candy Bomber* and *Chocolate Flyer.* His crewmates donated their rations and made parachutes out of handkerchiefs and clothing. Word spread, and other troops chipped in. Kids began writing letters to Tempelhof Airport, sending back the parachutes with special requests.

Halvorsen knew that any deviation from the basic mission wasn't allowed. Pilots were supposed to fly in a straight line from Rhein-Main to one of three airports on the free side of Berlin.

The commander of the Berlin Airlift was the humourless logistics genius William Tunner, a Major General with the Air Force, who worked eighteen hours a day and had no hobbies. Under his guidance, flights were landing almost every minute, around the clock. Halvorsen and his comrades faced disciplinary action after the piles of letters came to the attention of Tunner. Halvorsen was told to report to the commander. The young officer dreaded the meeting. To his delight, Tunner liked the good publicity and told him to carry on.

"Soon after, the Air Force officially adopted the name Operation Little Vittles for the candy drops and provided two German secretaries to deal with the mountain of fan mail," wrote Michael Tunnell in *Candy Bomber.* "It didn't take long for the crowds of kids and their parents to arrive at the end of the runway at Tempelhof. Crowds were too large … so he changed the parachute drops to random spots, such as parks, playgrounds, cemeteries and schoolyards. This led to letters from East Berlin children, because the Berlin Wall didn't exist, as yet. So children in the Soviet sector were dashing across the boundary to snap up a few parachutes."**

American companies began donating large quantities of their products. Individuals and groups also sent treats, as more pilots got involved in the special drops. Halvorsen was ordered to return to Mobile in January 1949, but others carried on until the end of the Airlift.

My mother's favourite story was about the movie *The Big Lift* which was filmed in Berlin in 1950, starring Montgomery Clift. The movie crew appeared on our street to film a segment of children waving at the airplanes and catching candy, falling from the sky. I was chosen as one of the children in this scene. When the movie was released we went to the theatre to watch it, but my mother was terribly disappointed when she didn't see the scene that was supposed to be my window to stardom. Perhaps it ended up on the cutting-room floor.

Blockading a city of 2.8 million people was conceived by evil minds. However, there was a show of determination, good will, ingenuity, love and compassion by people who had previously fought each other, a couple of years earlier, in a bitter war. This was indeed a great victory for humanity. There were many more crises to follow for Berlin until finally all Berliners were reunited on November 9, 1989.

Note: Excerpts and quotes were taken from articles previously published by Steven Benz, the Royal Air Force Museum, the Berlin Airlift Historical Foundation, Wikipedia.

* Gail Halvorsen's biography The Berlin Candy Bomber *(Horizon Publishers, 2002).*

** Michael O. Tunnell's Candy Bomber *(Charlesbridge, 2010).*

KONRAD BRINCK

Born in the 1940s in Berlin, Germany, Konrad Brinck immigrated to Canada in 1968 and had a career in sales. His stories appear in four anthologies, along with articles in ethnic German Magazines. Konrad lives in Brampton with his wife, and has one daughter and two grandchildren. His three books are *It's Just Me!; Trav-el-ations* and *A Nightmare Of A Trip Gone Bad.*

DORIS GRANT

Canadian War Cemetery
Beny-Sur-Mer, Reviers, France

"Slow down, Mom, our turn is coming up soon."

"Will it be a right or a left, Geoffrey?"

"It will be a right, and this is it!"

The tires crunched on the gravel as I slowed the car down to negotiate the turn.

"Hey Mom, I'm impressed. That was a neat turn. Now it should be just a few more kilometres from here. This countryside has stayed much the same since we left the coast, just cornfields and grazing land. It's actually hard to imagine a cemetery in the middle of this."

"Straight ahead, there seems to be a hedge coming up on the right."

Sure enough, a hedge had appeared, and it obstructed our view of the fields. It seemed to stretch quite a distance ahead and was set in from the road.

Thankfully, we noticed the road sign we'd been watching for. The Canadian War Cemetery, Beny-Sur-Mer, Reviers, was close by.

"Seems like we're the only ones here," Geoffrey said as we got out of the car.

"That's a plus for being off-season."

We walked across the parking lot and up three broad steps onto an expanse of well-groomed green grass. It was a large area that was surrounded by more of the hedge that we'd noticed from the road. In the distance, we could see what appeared to be a marble mausoleum, with a cross on top.

"Look Mom, they've planted maple trees here—a little bit of home, eh? That's a nice touch."

They were large maples too, probably planted when the cemetery was created, just after the war. Geoffrey was right, they were so familiar to us. As we moved through the grove, gradually the rows of gravestones became visible behind the mausoleum. We were shocked, as there were so many!

The entire cemetery was lovingly tended, with a row of colourful flowers growing at each grave. Between the rows of gravestones and flowers were swaths of well-tended grass. Surrounding the entire, spacious area was that carefully groomed hedge.

The first gravestone I saw bore the name and age of the buried soldier. I choked up and felt weak as I read "19 years of age." That's my son Geoffrey's age. At that very moment he said, "I'm going over to the other side, Mom."

We parted there, he veering to the left and I to the right.

Each gravestone bore a maple leaf, name, dates—often the age at death—and sometimes a short poem, such as:

"He gave his sweet red gift of life
That others could be free."

Or

"With a jest we left our home in the West
To die with the best. Now we rest."

My nose prickled and the back of my throat ached as I struggled with my emotions. How could one bear the loss of these young lives?

In the distance I could see Geoffrey, seemingly carefree with his ponytail blowing in the wind. I noticed, though, that he paused for long moments at some gravesides. I knew from his actions, the way he rubbed his hands together, kicked the ground and pressed one hand to his neck that he too, was struggling with strong emotions.

We wandered around for a long time, eventually meeting again at the mausoleum and walking back to the car together, not speaking. Under the maple trees he put his arm around my shoulders as we walked and gave me a squeeze. I gratefully hugged him to me, this precious, living nineteen year old.

DORIS GRANT

A Cold February Day

It had been a hard Ontario winter and the house on Queen Street was surrounded by several feet of snow. However, inside it was cozy with steady coal fires burning in the kitchen stove and Quebec heater in the front room. The kitchen, with its yellow walls, was the favourite room, and the table with its expanse of plaid oilcloth invited many activities. This morning Clara was busy making pastry on it.

"Momma, can I help?" little Joanie asked.

"Not right now. I have to make the pastry myself, but you can assist when I'm mixing the cake. All right?"

"Okay. I'll watch the cat."

The cat had settled in behind the stove for its morning nap, but Joanie crawled under and pulled him out. She then sat in the captain's chair beside the stove, her legs crossed, with her drowsy pet snuggled in her lap.

"Now, Mickey, you just stay here with me," she said as she petted him and ran her small fingers along his whiskers. He was a dark tabby, born in a litter of kittens their older cat had had two years earlier, and he had been a favourite with Joanie from the day he was born. He responded to her by nudging his face into her hand.

"Momma, why are you putting water on that stuff?"

"That's what you have to do with pastry, Joanie. You must have exactly the right amount, so you add just a bit at a time."

Joannie watched as Clara worked the dough on the breadboard.

"What are you going to make with it, Momma?"

"Well, I'm going to make an apple pie after the pastry has had a chance to rest for a while. We'll make our cake while I'm waiting."

Joanie's dark brown eyes took on a dreamy look as she caressed the cat and watched her mother's shoulders move up and down, coaxing the pastry into a workable mass. Clara wore one of her flowered, cotton housedresses (blue today) with a pink cotton apron over it—both of which she had made herself, as Joanie knew. Clara made all their clothes, perfectly, and Joanie loved being close to her like this. Now that her sisters were both in school, she and her mother spent entire days together.

"Momma, when will Dada be home again?"

"I don't know dear, soon I hope. It all depends on what the doctors say. Perhaps we'll get a letter today telling us when he'll be home."

"Is the hospital in Toronto big? Could he get lost there?"

"Yes, it's very big and they have special doctors who know exactly what to do when you're very sick—that's why your father is there. But no, he couldn't get lost, Joanie, the nurses and doctors watch everyone very carefully."

"I want him to come home."

"I do too, sweetheart. Now please put Mickey behind the stove and wash your hands. It's time for you to mix our cake up."

Joanie couldn't see the tears in her mother's eyes, but sensed her sadness and moved quickly to follow her orders. Clara used a dipper to put some warm water from the big pot on the stove into a basin in the sink, so Joanie didn't have to use the cold water from the tap. How she loved helping her mother mix things.

"Now bring over the small stool to stand on and let's get to work. I've already got the butter and sugar in the yellow bowl."

Joanie knew the drill. She stirred until the ingredients were soft and then, quick as a wink, her mother cracked in two eggs. She loved the way the eggs were at first quite separate from the mixture—the yellow yolks surrounded by the colourless liquid that her mother called "white." Then she put the spoon in the middle of each yolk and broke it, began slowly to stir and before long they had disappeared.

By now the mixture was very easy to stir, and she kept moving the spoon around while Clara added other things at intervals. She splashed a little when her mother poured the milk in.

"Now what comes next?"

"The flour of course, Momma, you know that."

Clara laughed as she sifted the flour.

"Pretty soon you'll be doing this all by yourself, won't you, Joanie?"

"Oh no, Momma, I only like doing it with you."

She watched her mother add a spoonful of white powder (called "baking powder") to the flour and then continued stirring as Clara gradually added the flour to the batter. It became more difficult for Joanie to stir, but she soldiered on, knowing it would get easier once the flour was mixed in.

"Would you like chocolate today, Joanie?"

"Oh yes, please."

Once Clara added cocoa, the batter changed quickly from white to dark brown, and Joanie began to think about licking the spoon. She hoped her mother wouldn't notice the milk and flour she had somehow splashed from the bowl earlier.

While she continued stirring, her mother cut wax paper to line the cake pan and neatly fitted it into place. Then she took the bowl from Joanie and poured the batter into the lined pan, taking care to clean and scrape the bowl as best she could.

"Now dear, it's time to put this in the oven. Would you please finish off the bowl and spoon for me?"

Joanie spent considerable time getting the remaining batter from the bowl, using the spoon at first. She concluded by running her fingers around the inside of the bowl and licking its edges.

"Momma, I love helping you bake," she said, and settled happily into the chair beside the stove.

DORIS GRANT

Doris Grant has a Master's Degree in English from the University of Western Ontario, and taught English and Art History for almost 30 years at Georgian College in Barrie. Now retired, she enjoys writing about her travels and family history. She lives and writes in Mississauga.

TASNIM JIVAJI

Clear

Clear sat cross-legged sifting the sand between her fingers, her face tilted up, scrunched, as if blissfully listening to a wonderful piece of music. In reality she was just too hungry and was actually feeling dizzy. Her long hair blew freely in the breeze as the sunlight cast a dust halo around her.

There she sat, all alone, nesting as usual on the soft beach sand which kept her warm. If anyone ever wanted to find her, they would look for her here, but then again no one ever looked for her and never would. Her name was Clear, she was given that name because the woman who might have been her mother said they were invisible, and that was the reason why people did not see them. The woman had disappeared a long time ago leaving Clear all by herself on the beach.

At times, when Clear gazed into the water, she would see herself reflected as clear and as transparent as the water itself. Only then she would feel as though she belonged. This was her home. There weren't any walls surrounding her. The view was the panorama that spanned all the way to that faraway place, which was the horizon. That's where the sun slid under the line which separated the water from the sky, displaying two cascading colours of blue. The endless ribbon of sand and ocean appeared to be the sides of her home, and there was one real wall she considered to be the back of her home. This was a tall slab of concrete that offered shelter on windy days. Clear would huddle up against this wall and feel the cold concrete press against her back, through her burlap dress.

Noises caught her attention and she stood up looking expectantly in the direction of that distant, fenced off location where people often gathered to have a picnic and enjoy themselves. Often children's laughter came floating like jingles in the air. She followed the sound stealthily until she was standing a few paces away from the fence. Standing there, silently watching them with soft child-like eyes. Today, there was a crowd, a family, and they occupied all the picnic tables in the enclosure. Their colourful clothes added to the decorations that had been placed on the tables of the simple space. The area was shaded by a huge, old mango tree.

She scanned their happy faces and realized they were celebrating a special occasion. Waiters moved between tables, with respectful flair as they laid down the large platters of food. The women fussed over each other and the men were jovially nodding approval on tasting the well prepared meal. They were generously pouring each other drinks. A little girl in an angel-blue, frilly dress, excitedly clapped her hands at seeing the brightly decorated unicorn cake being brought to her table. She was busy telling her friends some stories. She clumsily hit her glass of juice with her elbow, but no one noticed. The drink flooded the table and dripped away down the edge, getting soaked up by the soil underneath.

No one at the party saw Clear standing there watching them enjoying themselves. Eventually she grew weary and she sadly went back to her little mold in the sand. She hugged herself and rested her forehead on her knees. She felt a sickly loneliness pricking her throat. Many times, she had watched people gathered together like this, and she wondered what it was like to have a family and friends.

Long ago, Clear had asked the woman who could have been her mother, what it was like for her to socialize with so many people. The woman had not replied. She simply gave a contemplative shrug and shook her head. She was absorbed in her own thoughts, leaving Clear to wonder where all these people lived. She often spied on her nearby neighbours, the folks who lived in houses along her beach. Clear had never seen the inside of their homes—she only knew that the beach was her home and she knew nothing about the rest of the world: those who lived in their stone cages. Whether it rained or was the hottest of days ... or the darkest of nights, when the sky gave her so much light ... she could see the stars in the heavenly sky, blinking amongst themselves. This was the only world she knew.

Clear heard a sputtering sound and looked up to see four fishermen in their boat so close to the sand that it was nearly going to become beached. She had seen these boats often on the shore drifting toward their jetties, after a day out to sea. However, this boat was not going anywhere. It just bobbed about, like a seagull sitting in the waves. The fishermen were waving to someone on the beach. Clear did not look at who they were waving at as it didn't matter to her anyway. They didn't even know she was there, she believed.

Then, one fisherman jumped out of the boat and, splashing in the knee-high water, came toward the shore. He had a fish in his hands and it was wiggling about trying to escape the grasp that was holding it out of its element. Now the fisherman stood in front of her and offered Clear the fish. Confused, she looked up at the fisherman and then at the fish not knowing what to do with his gift. He knelt down, left the fish on the sand beside her and ran back to his boat. Clear held her breath as she watched him go, she wanted to hold the fishy, sweaty smell of the fisherman a little bit longer in her nostrils, lingering in the closeness of someone near her.

The fish slapped about and Clear looked at it blankly. She didn't know what to do with it. She could see that the fish was looking at her while it struggled to breathe. Moreover, Clear was startled by the closeness of it. It was lovely and colourful with its scales glistening in hues of greens, yellows and blues. What was Clear to do with this beauty? She saw that the life of the fish was leaving it with every breath it was trying to take. She picked the fish up gently, cradling it to her bosom and she walked to the water's edge. The fish became calm in their embrace and when she lowered it into the water, it paused to look up at her and then swiftly darted away, instantaneously disappearing in the azure blueness.

Did the fisherman think that she would make a meal of the fish? How could she? Clear could never ever end the life of so beautiful a fish as this one. She waited to see if the fish came back, but it did not. She wondered where it lived in the water? What did its home look like? Did it live with a family who lived amongst a school of others?

This little fish reminded Clear of the small girl at the party who was chattering away telling her friends her cute little stories. Would the fish tell the adventure story of how it was carried to land and visited a girl on the beach? Or, Clear wondered sadly, did it live alone? All by itself in the vast ocean? Maybe Clear would see it again playing in the waves that lapped and teased her when she dipped herself in the crystal blue sea.

TASNIM JIVAJI

An artist, a writer, a mother, a constant work-in-progress in becoming human. Tasnim Jivaji continues to be the same kid from Mombasa, inside, from where the seeds of her stories and art grow. She considers herself the luckiest of beings to have the chance to own her God-given gifts and to share them with others.

LINDA CASSIDY

Something-Other-Than: Memoir of a Singularity
Prologue

For a significant portion of my life, I yearned for something that had no name. For a long time, I couldn't shake off the feeling that I was missing a special knowledge shared by others but not by me. If only I looked hard enough and long enough, I too might possess the key to an invisible yet glorious vault where something special awaited me. Growing up an only child reinforced my feeling of being a singular entity, self-contained, alone but not necessarily lonely, seeking a way to link up with the universal singularity.

This yearning and sense of singularity was not caused by adverse circumstances in my life. On the contrary, I have had a very good life—a secure childhood, an enduring marriage, two caring sons, and an intellectually challenging career. I've never missed a meal because the pantry was bare or needed to worry about making the next mortgage payment. Until recently, my physical body has carried me through life with relative ease and grace and my mind has, for the most part, been able to handle the demands placed on it.

Of course, I've not been spared the darker emotions of anger, jealousy, insecurity, and depression released when my needs and desires were not accommodated by my close circle of singularities. While the resulting pangs of disappointment and unhappiness swirled around me like mosquitos on a hot summer night, they soon faded away. Only a few itchy punctures remained behind on my psychic skin, but they were not the cause of any long running traumas.

Most fortunate of all, I've been spared the extreme symptoms of unhappiness such as physical, emotional, and substance abuse that can shatter a life into a million pieces. Yes, I've had a good life.

I don't take full credit for this good fortune. I never had a master plan for how I would conduct myself to reach a pre-determined goal. It was just how events unfolded over the decades. A missed opportunity, an encounter with violence or a major illness, any number of fateful occurrences could have changed the trajectory of this good fortune. The missing dimension in my existence, it seemed, was unrelated to the particulars of my personal life.

When I consciously began to seek out this missing dimension, I realized it sounded suspiciously like the start of the ubiquitous search for God. I didn't like to define this dimension by the word "God." As history has shown, conflicting views on how to be with God can trigger terrible wars. I wanted my own label for the divine, untainted by the perceptions of others. One day, an appropriate label was delivered to me in a poem I wrote about a group of skiers sitting around a fire in a ski lodge. In the last line of the second verse a descriptive phrase popped out unbidden from my imagination:

> *"Let's ski the night," you said.*
> *The invitation sounded perfect*
> *to the time. I recall we balanced*
> *on a sofa lumpier than most*
> *and chatted over/under*
> *the voices of twenty/thirty more.*
> *Green-skinned logs shot amber bullets*
> *at our squared-off boots*
> *and the maple smoke wooed*
> *my sugar longing for something-other-than.*

> Linda Cassidy, *Inland Waterways: Poems*
> *From A Peaceable Kingdom,* 2010

Something-Other-Than ... that phrase grabbed my attention. In the poem the scent of burning logs had triggered that inner yearning which my imagination promptly labeled as *Something-Other-Than*. While the phrase was very non-specific, I liked the vagueness as it gave space for whatever I might find on my quest without the strictures of the traditional religions.

I was under no illusion of being the first to experience such yearnings. For millennia philosophers, mystics, poets, and psychologists have tried to crack open the mystery of human existence. What exactly does it mean to participate in a life on Planet Earth and, in the end, to depart from it forever with no knowledge of our ultimate destination? This presents a huge challenge for a singularity like myself to go off on my own to discover the mystery of the universe. Perhaps it could be interpreted by those raised in the traditional faiths of Christianity, Islam, and Hinduism as an act of supreme hubris. After all, for over thousands of years many wise priests and prophets have written sacred texts about the divine. As well, they have established clerical hierarchies and spiritual rituals with guidelines to help seekers navigate the razor's edge of finding God. Who was I to think I would discover a wisdom on my own, that the great prophets had missed?

The reason I took it upon myself to redo what has been tried for centuries, was the inability of existing religious orthodoxies to fulfill that yearning in me, to connect me with my soul, my spiritual nature. It was not enough to rely solely on the words and experience of others. Why, I felt, should something essential to the wellbeing and evolution of humankind be kept a dark secret, open only to the chosen few? I didn't want to take the word of others claiming to have discovered God. I wanted the bedrock of my spiritual life to come through my personal experience. Until I discovered a deeper guideline for living, I would abide by the Golden Rule: Do unto others as you would have done unto you. This rule extends back to Ancient Egypt and was cited by Christ in one of his sermons. The virtue of kindness embedded in the Golden Rule would keep me on the path of love, respect, and peace in dealing with others.

As I reach my eightieth decade, I want to share the story of how I went about my spiritual quest as a singularity. I hope my sightings of *Something-Other-Than* will resonate with sightings by other singularities. In this memoir I will relate how in my search I pursued the ways of books, yoga, poetry, and dreams and what I learned from each pathway.

We rarely speak of the divine to each other fearing to open ourselves to ridicule. I believe a willingness and ability to express our discovered truths, if done well and honouring the truth of others, can contribute to a deeper understanding of the world of soul and spirit. Sharing our spiritual sightings in all their diversity can build greater respect for one another and tear down the walls of spiritual strife that generate such terrible conflict in the world.

Note: This Prologue excerpt is from Linda Cassidy's soon to be published book, Something-Other-Than: Memoir of a Singularity.

LINDA CASSIDY

Linda Cassidy is a poet and prose writer. Her poetry collection, *Inland Waterways: Poems from a Peaceable Kingdom*, highlights moments in the ebb and flow of a woman's inner life. Her mystery novel, *The Long Revenge*, is a story of betrayal and revenge between two sisters. Linda's work-in-progress is titled *Something-Other-Than: Memoir of a Singularity*.

VERSE

PRATAP REDDY

Okänd Konstnär
Discovering an Artist in Gothenburg

Golden sunshine pours down
From a sky blue and blameless

    Spring is everywhere,
    On the streets and in the parks,
    Even at the museum, even in my step!

But winter, that clinging persistent lover,
Hangs around in the Kattegat Sound,
Waving her frozen hand at every chance.

    The Fürstenberg Gallery,
    Had hung artists, nailing them to the wall,
    Punishing them for daring
    To bring Beauty into our lives.

Sumptuous bodies, fleshed out by Rubens,
And the great Rembrandt at pains
To paint himself over and over again.
Impressionist images drenched in sun,
And sudsy seas burned in Turner's vision.

    (When I went to the loo
    I found Jackson Pollock, too)
    What caught my eye, was this local guy:

Amazingly versatile, Swedish to the core.
Okänd Konstnär's the name he bore.
He filled the place with canvasses galore
Still Life, Landscapes, Abstract and more.

Who was this man I'd never heard of before?
A master, it appears, of every known school of art.

When my cousin turned up in his true-blue Volvo
I gushed about this Scandinavian maestro
"Okänd Konstnär, you mutton-head,
Is Swedish for Unknown Artist," he said.

PRATAP REDDY

Karma's Child

I lie belly up on the sands of Time,
beside the Ocean, whose incessant waves
tirelessly murmur, *Aum, Aum, Aum*

Beyond the knife-thin horizon,
where the sea meets the sky,
in a tight embrace,
there circles a school of sharks,
baring their sword-sharp teeth
as if smiling at me.

No laughing matter,
when I've to step into the water –
a fleshy tidbit I'll be,
so says Peter Benchley,
for those gigantic, masticating *Jaws*

O, Sun! Helios, Ra, Savitr, or whatever,
forgive me my many transgressions.
But the day of judgement's near –
Is there room for plea bargains?

In my declining years, adrift and bereft,
my stash of good deeds now come to nought.
A thousand prayers die on my lips.
For my throat is parched, sore for a dose
of something spiritual, of something sublime.

A frosted glass of margarita with extra lime,
and salt encrusting the brim,
like the accretion of karmic sin.

One sip, and everything will be fine.
A couple of rounds will make it divine.

Who cares for Tomorrow or the day after?
Death or Nirvana, for that matter,

Today's bad enough.

Don't stand there and pontificate –
Just buy me a drink (even a beer will do).

PRATAP REDDY

WRITER'S BLOCK

Chipping away
At the immense mass in my head
fruitlessly –
The characters refuse to come to life;
Dead dialogue congeals in their mouths

I lay down the tools; sitting idle,
Whiling away the empty hours,
I stare out of my high-rise window –

In the distance, slumming with Lake Ontario
Is Toronto
    It's late in the evening,
    the CN Tower
    looks like an upright python
    that has swallowed up a flying saucer.

When night falls, a gulf of darkness separates us;
but the ground is a throw of black satin with sequins;
some gold, some silver, some red,
flowing in endless processions,
like regimented glow-worms.

    In the fall, the autumnal colours singe the city –
    A frozen forest fire!
    While the Tower stands tall,
    Basking in lucid light of day,

Un-mindful of the reminders from the lake
about winter skulking round the corner.

When winter arrives –
the landscape becomes a sepia print
brown houses and dirty snow.
A few firs, refusing to go with the flow,
stand out like exclamations marks
The Tower, shivering behind a veil of haze
Disappears, and reappears
whimsically;
the lifeless lake has become
one with the sky.

    Is there a sharp chisel or
    a sharper pencil?
    Or some other magical
    utensil
    My incomparable wit
    perhaps, or my lively
    imagination
    That will galvanise the
    cadavers of my fiction?

CN Tower - Watercolour by Pratap Reddy

But tonight –
The long lonely barren vigil
is coming to an end – behold!
The first fingers of light are applying colour,
Pink, purple and gold,
to the underbellies of the clouds.

The urgent predawn chidings of birds
float up to my window like radio static
of a program that could well be *Good Morning, Canada!*

    The stars – turning their backs on the newborn day –
    look so lovely in the final throes of the night.

The sun rises –
a vermillion daub, on the forehead of the day.
Forming a glorious halo behind the Tower,
And radiating benedictions upon this earth.

In the dark the crypt of creativity,
A tiny spark flutters,
slowly growing into a flaming torch –
my votive offering to the begrudging muses.
The mellow light shines
 in every benighted recess.
Then I hear a sound;
And I see and sense a movement.

My characters are beginning to stir.
And my hopeful trembling hand,
reaches for the keys of my computer.

In that resplendent hour,
sharp as a stylus, the CN Tower
is writing a prayer in the sky.

PRATAP REDDY

Pratap Reddy moved to Canada from India. An underwriter by day, writer by night, he writes fiction, and poetry. An alumnus of Humber School for Writers, he's the author of *Weather Permitting & Other Stories* (2016) and *Ramya's Treasure* (2018). A recipient of the Marty award for Literary Arts (2021), he lives in Mississauga with his wife and son.

GEETA KRISHNAMOORTHY

Claptrap and Balderdash

I talk of crochet and tatting lace
Reading poetry by the fireplace
Or of a river in spring
And you think
Oh, it's claptrap and balderdash!

I share the thrill of feeling great
On entering a holy space
Or of the divine heights I ascend
As music takes me on a high
And you say
Oh, that's tripe and balderdash!

I speak of vibrant colours
Merging inwards, brilliant hues
In my mind's eye, when I meditate
Of auras and healing vibes
And you cry
Oh, that's poppycock and balderdash!

Of magic weaves and melodies
Of vibrant leaves on deciduous trees
Of nature's beauty in changing climes
Of reading thoughts from another time
Of music and mirth where minds meet
And handwritten letters, oh what a treat

And you decry
Oh, that's hogwash and balderdash!

Stocks and shares, malls and soothing spas
To melt your corporate cholesterol
Fast cars, labels and staying on top
Retail therapy – to unwind, just shop
Branded goods, prized memberships
Caviar, wine and exotic dips
All this may float your boat
But for me, just give me
My claptrap and balderdash!

For…
What floats your boat
Just gets my goat!

GEETA KRISHNAMOORTHY

The Abandoned Trolley

There I lie on my side
On the grass beside the sidewalk
Like a beast of burden
Past my prime, spent
Discarded, abandoned
Left exposed to the elements
And the air is rent
With silent screams
From my abuse.

Once part of a glorious
Line of trolleys
People paid for my company
And me – my good deed done for the day,
Having embraced and carried
The needs of a family,
Returned to the fold
Ensconced, clasped
By my own family.

Until kidnapped by a
Two-legged monster, who,
With values akilter
Took me away from my safe haven

And who discovered
That upon reaching home and
Unloading me
Had no more use for me
Surreptitiously, in the night,
As if leaving behind a bag of body parts
Left me lying
Helpless on
This grassy patch.

GEETA KRISHNAMOORTHY

Crane and Mouse

Sounds like a legal house
But no, this is an ode
To two women
To whom much is owed.

Two women, both petite
Just shy of five feet
Born seven years apart
Each with a golden heart
So much in common
Physically, mentally
A story of lives lived selflessly…

Sheela Basrur
"Mighty Mouse"

Close cropped hair
Matter of fact, a no-nonsense air
Sleeves rolled up
Ever ready for challenges
That life and work threw at them
Battling…
Disease and Discrimination
Infection and Injustice
Contamination and Corruption

Kiran Bedi
"Crane"

One fought a deadly virus that flew in
Snatching away peace of mind and safety

Sheela, meaning good conduct or character
Carrying the city on her small shoulders
Heralding hope in times of despair

The other relegated to tend a hopeless prison
True to her name, Kiran
Bringing light and reformation
Through meditation.

SARS and Tihar
Could not beat this pair
Two women, both diminutive
Standing tall in everyone's perspective
Amazing Amazons, they are
"Mighty Mouse" Basrur and "Crane" Bedi.

Sheela Basrur (1956-2008) was Ontario Chief Medical Officer of Health and Assistant Deputy Minister of Public Health, and led the fight against the SARS virus. (Pic: Courtesy of Basrur family.)

Kiran Bedi, India's first female police officer, earned the epithet Crane for towing an illegally parked vehicle of the Prime Minister. Years later in Tihar, a notorious jail for hardened criminals, she brought about remarkable reforms. (Bedi's photo by A. Manikandan — used under the Creative Commons Attribution-Share Alike 4.0 International license/Wikimedia.)

GEETA KRISHNAMOORTHY

Touchy-feely wordy wench
pens poems when she feels the wrench
Of a thought, an emotion, a hug, a scent -
the memory of a life well spent.

Anything that brings a smile — spring in the walk, heel-clicking in midair happiness, something to visit and revisit and enjoy. The pore-permeating Goodness of being alive.

SERINA LEWIS

Singer

Black with a gold monogram
that contained the letter "S"
for Serina? Or for Singer.
It remained gold and shiny
for as long as I can remember.
The machine rested on a wooden base.
When Mum lifted off the hardboard cover
we knew the magic would begin.

  She'd tip the machine back to check
  the bobbin, thread the needle, adjust the tension
  in order to match it with the fabric.
  With her agile foot on the motor
  her right hand controlling the wheel
  it began to sing, as it rolled along
  creating a very special garment.

The base contained the bobbin.
She had a tiny piece of lint, free
fabric and machine oil for greasing
the electrical engine's moving parts.
Shirts and skirts magically appeared,
more frocks with frills
complete with delicate collars and cuffs.
High fashions that were fit for a runway.

Every fabric was pinned and tacked
according to her custom-made pattern
that she'd meticulously craft herself
using yesterdays' newspaper.
With every twist and turn of the master's baton
she would re-imagine the silks and satin
and cottons into an amazing fashion statement
for her three girls and for a future generation
especially for her *malgodi's little Anysha Angel
and Divi Doll.

For decades, she rolled into bundles
remnants of fabric, sorted by color or pattern
to be cut and squared and pieced together for
a patchwork quilt
creating an heirloom that would be so cherished
it would be a memory maker for years to come,
plus, the quilt would be a conversation starter.
That would begin with the inevitable, "Do you remember that
pillow, pyjama, cushion cover, coat, dress or drape...?"
And the Singer's song would continue on ♪♪♪♪

* Malgodi means the eldest daughter in our "mother tongue" Konkani.

SERINA LEWIS

The Circle

They gather around the circle
the maker of music
   the weaver of tales
      the grinder of spices
         the tiller of rice fields
            the adventurer who sailed the seven seas
               ancestors who walked barefoot or in humble *chappals*

they congregate by the fire
to stoke the flames of the hearts
of those still in the Earth's realm.
Wandering this *sansaar* are…
          the artists
             the writers
               the soldiers
                 the bankers
                    the teachers
                the engineers
             the thinkers
dhonnobad to all those who serve the human family.

Let us not forget…
the herbal healers
      the toddy tappers
         the tireless helpers
            the singers of *mandos*

the soothers of the lonely
　　the dreamers from foreign shores
　　　　the birthers of successive generations
　　　　　　the youth who wrote letters for their elders

each one leaving footprints indelible on Mother Earth.

To the Ancient ones…
　　Spirit Guides
　　Forefathers and Foremothers
waiting to welcome home, my soul
enlarging the ever-widening sphere
the circle with no definite circumference
around the primordial fire at its heart.

　　　　　　　　　　　　Miigwech Chi-Miigwech

Legend:
Chappals: Flip-flops in Hindi
Sansaar: World in Hindi
Dhonnobad: Thanks in Bengali
Mandos: Folk songs of Goa, India
Miigwich Chi-Miigwich: Thanks, Many Thanks in Ojibwa

SERINA LEWIS

A retired educator, Serina Lewis is an aspiring writer and poet. As a teacher she enjoyed working with children. She is a yoga instructor with a love of nature, people and places reflected in her writing. A passion for listening and self-expression drive her art, music and written word. Her goal is to be a lifelong learner.

ROY MARQUES

Falling

Left me dreaming, softly speaking
Sunshine above our heads,
in the summertime.
Left fragment flowers, by the trails of Erindale
It's the summer of our times
It's the summer of disguise

Left me wishing,
slowly walking
Slowly Falling, Falling.
It's the summer of our times
It's the summer of disguise

St. Peter's Church, in Erindale, (Mississauga) - Roy Marques

Left me dreaming
Softly speaking
Sunshine above our heads
By the beauty left unsaid

Left me wanting
Wanting to be near
Whisper in your ear
How I'm Falling, Falling

It's the summer of our times
It's the summer of disguise
And the summer of our lives
It's the summer of disguise

For M.B.

ROY MARQUES

Mallory

By your lovely skin
I remember everything
Everything
As the sun moves in
As your life begins
Mallory, Mallory

And the song I sing
And the joy you bring
Joy you bring
Such a lovely thing
Lovely thing

As the dark descends
And the rain begins
The admiration begins
Mallory, Mallory

La, La, La, La (x5)
Away you are
Beneath the Stars
Mallory, Mallory

ROY MARQUES

Shoreline

There is a space in her heart
Where everything always shines
Always happy, never sad
The memories rise up in the mornings

On the shoreline
Content in our minds
And the swans keep gliding
By the shoreline

I can see it in her eyes
Something bright exists from long ago
By the river near the trees
When she arrives, next to me

By the shoreline
Captivated by her beautiful mind
As the clouds keep drifting
By the shoreline
At the edge of a dream
I think of you
By the shoreline

And as I walk down the trails
To be where everyone stays apart
By the beating of thy heart

So every day, I see your image
As the current swiftly passes

There is a place in her heart
Where everything always shines
Always happy, seldom sad

By the shoreline
And the sun is always bright
By the shoreline
If only in dreams
I think of you
By the shoreline
Looking over the edge
I swim to you
By the shoreline

For M.B.

ROY MARQUES

Roy Marques is a cinematographer and based in Mississauga, working on 35 mm film. Marques is photographing *In Memory*, a short film influenced by Chris Marker, *La Jetee*. He enjoys writing lyrics and short stories. *www.csc.ca*

IVY REISS

Living In Your Shadow

I like living in your shadow
it is better with than without
and if I must choose
from one of the two
I would choose you

You cast a light
as if the sun shines
wherever you look
and although it is cold
when you look away
it is still not as cold
as when you've gone away

I see that in your shadow
there is still warmth
if only in knowing
I am by your side
close enough to fall
into your shadow

For it is true
all that shines
casts darkness too

IVY REISS

Save Your Self

Remember
There is a world out there
Waiting. Living. Breathing.
There are eyes and faces and smiles
There are people, embraces, and warm places
It is there
Out there
And you—you are in here

If you can go
If you can make it
Out There
Somewhere
Someone
Will be there

This is not beyond your reach—
It is just beyond the window pane.
There is light
There is air
There is love
But you must go
Go now!
You can find it

Save Your Self
If you stay in here, it will end
It's pressing and taking all that you have
Be strong
Be brave
Go!
Before it's too late

Note: *"Living in your Shadow" and "Save Your Self" are excerpts from* There is a Place, *in the complete collection, published by Aeolus House.*

IVY REISS

Rackets

We were always in the moment,
We talked about past stories,
We talked about the world and how it may go forward,
We talked about the houses, the sky, the people,
We talked about the parks, music, bike rides, and art,
We talked about things we would like to do,
could do, and might do.
We talked about things we had done, places we'd been,
places we'd like to go visit, and things we may do again.

We talked of many ideas
and how they could come to fruition,
We talked about where we would like to be
and ways we may get there.
These walks were at the end of long days,
days full of delicious food,
warmth and laughter.

This was in the spring time.
When summer opened up
we rode our bikes instead,
fished by the waters, laughed out loud,
sang songs and explored the city.
We did many of the things we had talked about,
and our talks and dreams seemed to evolve for a time.

Then, as the slightest chill came into the air,
and August folded into September,
the bike rides stopped, as had the walks.

Late fall approached, the other night
we walked, I mentioned
how warm the weather was—
But you went on about the rackets,
as I held your hand.

"Rackets" by Ivy Reiss, published here first, exclusively in the Courtney Park Writers' Group anthology Crazy Cove.

IVY REISS

Ivy Reiss is the founding publisher/editor/art director of The Artis Media Network. Her collection, *There is a Place* (Aeolus House; imprint of Quattro Books) launched December 2020. She remains in demand as a culture writer, speaker, event-coordinator, and host. Contact via TheArtisMagazine.com and IvyReiss.com. Follow on FB *@ArtisMagazine* & Twitter *@Ivy_Reiss*

JOANN WANDA ROSSITTER

Riverwood Tree Stump

As I walk in the beautiful forest,
I stop beside a lump and a bump in the deep green glade,
Where there is a clump of dried leaves and new growth…
I look at this very old stump of an ancient tree.

I see the playful black and grey squirrels,
As they jump from tree to tree in the branches above…
I listen to the birds singing sweetly.
I hear the nearby stream flowing
   over rocks and dead branches.

I walk along the banks of the muddy river,
I also hear the beat of the thump and whomp,
Of the tails of the frisky brown beavers,
      working away on their den,
I love my joyful walk in the peaceful forest.

JOANN WANDA ROSSITTER

Flowers and Fish

Pink flowers and fish,

Lovely, fluffy and fertile,

Wild and Pink and Black.

JOANN WANDA ROSSITTER

La Solitude
(French translation)

Solitude
(English version)

Quand je me trouve,

Dans la solitude de ma chambre.

Et comme je regarde partout,

Ce qu'il y a de beau dedans.

Rien ne me donne plus de joie,

Que le beau cadeau de toi.

Car sans toi à côté de moi,

Je me trouve tout perdue,

Plus que je n'ai jamais cru,

… tu me manques beaucoup!

When I find myself,

In the solitude of my room.

And I look out to see,

All the beauty around me.

Nothing gives me the same joy,

As the gift of your presence.

Because, without you by my side,

As I abide, I feel all alone,

More than I ever thought,

… I miss you a lot!

JOANN WANDA ROSSITTER

Wanda is a Toronto-born artist. She spent many years as an English, French and Special Education teacher. She loves to sing, dance and create visual arts, and has received several awards. She has written two novellas and various poems. Wanda attained a Master's degree in Theology from the University of Toronto. She enjoys being an active volunteer in Mississauga.

MEENA CHOPRA

The Deep Dark Woods

She strolls on the blue moons, dead stars, aging regions
glaciers and valleys.
Sauntering on curvatures in a distant strange land
meandering a digressed wilderness.

The deep dark woods deluged her eyes.

Subdivided, she turns around,
walks back towards her homeland.
Stepping into the courtyard
she sits on the doorstep
feels safe and sheltered
squeezing the setting sun
in her squinted eyes.

The dusk, silent and in-tuned
silhouettes stretched,
sprawling on the barren dark walls.

And then,
a moonbeam stumbles down
softly thresholding her anatomy.
Recharged and refreshed
her stark naked soul frontlines and moves ahead
once again rejoicing and dancing
as she dawns in a new day.

Thousands of days break in her eyes.

An eternal traveler, she turns around,
to catch up with an untrodden trail,
ready to walk miles again to an unknown forest
she reaches her roots to rise again.

The deep dark woods fire her eyes.

Days, years and eons passed by
The deep dark woods were lost in her sight

MEENA CHOPRA

Cybernetic Reality Tunneled in Time

Night locked, neon's blinking
lurching on the floundering grounds of reality
clinging to a driftwood
surfing on the roaring mountain waves
pulled in the ocean's gravity,
ripples swirl away from my shoulders
foaming and sweeping fragmented replicants
clutching to a sinking saviour
these cyberpunks spall
islanding the surcharged divinities

Between me and myself
is there no blade runner?
Between the dots and the lines
are there no interludes?
Between the sky and the sea
is there no shore?
Between the sound and the music
is there no symphony?
Between the moon and the sun
is there no asteroid and a shooting star?
Between the day and the night
is there no whirling fire-fly?

Between the life and the death
is there no trace of breath?
Between the cause and its effect
is there no simmering karma?
Between sanctum and sanctorum
is there no mindfulness?
Between the anima and the animus
is there no androgynous *ardhanarishvara**
Between Venus and Mercury
is there no hermaphroditic homogeneity?
And
Between the blade and the blade runner
is there no personified emancipator?

Or,
Is it –

Just a remote piercing gaze
lasering off the decayed and the old
the container and the contained
edging around the razor?

A burning
stifled, timorous mirage
circuiting a hallucinating nihility.

An excavated future
tunneled in time!

* *Composite androgenous Hindu deity, a symbolic unity of nature and knowledge.*

MEENA CHOPRA

Footsteps of the Sky

I glimpsed your footsteps
gliding over the sky-sphere
piercing the seamless folklores
orbiting rambling images
and then
stepping down
through the circled downdraft.

Grounding the morning breeze
cooling the calm earth
hugging an untamed blue yonder.
Desert sand captures the fleeting clouds
The life halts
savours a few cherished moments
gazing over the wild wasteland.

Footsteps of the sky twitter,
lingering over the treetops
forever.

MEENA CHOPRA

Meena Chopra is a poet and a visual artist: emigrated from India, now lives in Mississauga, Canada. She has authored three poetry collections and co-edited one anthology. She writes both in English and her native Hindi language. Amongst many accolades, she has been awarded for her distinguished work in literature and art by the National Ethnic Press and Media Council of Canada. *www.meenachopra-artist.com*

www.ingramcontent.com/pod-product-compliance
Lightning Source LLC
Chambersburg PA
CBHW030336020726
47493CB00004B/1299